C000255641

ANNA'S PROMISE
THE MAREN BAY SERIES
BOOK II

PAULINE TAIT

FOUNTAINBRIDGE
PUBLISHING

This edition is published in 2024 by Fountainbridge Publishing
Text copyright © Pauline Tait 2024
www.paulinetait.com

The right of Pauline Tait to be identified as the author of this work
has been asserted in accordance with the Copyright, Designs and
Patents Act 1988 Sections 77 and 78.

All rights reserved. No part of this publication may be reproduced,
stored in a retrieval system, or transmitted in any form or by any
means, electronic, mechanical, photocopying, recording or otherwise,
without prior permission of the copyright holder.

This is a work of fiction. Names, characters, places and incidents
either are products of the author's imagination or are used fictitiously.
Any resemblance to actual events or locales or persons, living or dead,
is entirely coincidental.

ISBN 978-1-7392443-3-0 (paperback)
ISBN 978-1-7392443-2-3 (ebook)

THE MAREN BAY SERIES

The stunning Scottish Isle of Skye forms the backdrop to this suspenseful mystery series that's not short on romance. From new beginnings and second chances to love conquering over loss and deception, The Maren Bay series introduces 'authentically dynamic characters with whom readers develop an immediate connection.'
'Masterfully complex and intriguing tales of love, loyalty, betrayal and subterfuge' that will keep readers on edge throughout the series.

Abigail Returns (The Maren Bay Series Book 1)
Anna's Promise (The Maren Bay Series Book 2)

ACKNOWLEDGMENTS

Researching for the next novel is a crucial part of a writer's process and one I enjoy. But it is often bolstered by the willingness of those we reach out to, as their generosity with both time and information can make such a difference to the accuracy of our writing.

With that in mind, I would like to thank Catherine MacPhee, Archivist at the Skye & Lochalsh Archive Centre in Portree, and Maressa Munro, Crofter at Feorlig, Isle of Skye.

G.J. Kemp, fellow author and techy whiz who has come to my rescue on numerous occasions when I've lost in my battles with technology.

And finally, and quite simply, to my husband. A constant source of strength and encouragement.

CHAPTER ONE

Tossing her camera onto the passenger seat, Anna gasped for breath. Her hands shaking, she fumbled her key into the ignition before thrusting her old jeep into first, moving quickly through the gears as she sped down the hill. Looking back, she strained to see through the cloud of dust churned up from the dirt track beneath. He had seen her. She knew that for sure. But who was he, and why was he there?

Thirty minutes later, having driven the road less travelled by tourists from Struan to Portree, Anna could feel her panic waning. Portree was by far her favourite place on the island. She'd been visiting the Isle of Skye since she was a little girl, but this time was different, and she was beginning to question whether her love for the island came, perhaps, from a deeper place. Was there more to the Isle of Skye for Anna than the stunning scenery and friends she'd made along the way?

Parking by the harbour, Anna gazed out across the glistening water. A sailing boat leaving the calmness of the sheltered water meandered out into the Sound of Raasay. While the top of the Cuillins were shrouded in cloud, just as they had been when she'd driven into Portree that morning. It was a view she loved. A view that, although ever-changing, unfailingly filled her with a sense of calm.

Slipping her camera into her ruck sack, she thought about the man she'd seen earlier. She had questions, and lots of them, but no one to ask. The only thing she could do was study the photographs she'd taken earlier, before she'd had to leave in such a hurry. And she knew she needed to re-read her mother's letter. Maybe there was something she'd missed.

Crossing the road towards The Water's Edge, Anna couldn't help but smile. She stepped aside to allow a group of well-fed tourists to leave the restaurant, ready to embark on their evening's walk. Mouth-watering aromas greeted Anna before she was through the door.

'Hey, *Susie*! Come on in. I've an empty table by the fire just waiting for you.'

In front of the roaring flames, a dog was curled up making the most of the heat, and Anna could feel herself relaxing as she took off her winter layers.

'Thank you, Rob. Can I park myself here for the evening or do you need the table later?'

'*Susie, Susie, Susie,* you sit there for as long as you like. I'll bring you a coffee in a sec.'

Watching Rob's larger-than-life personality disappear behind the packed bar, Anna couldn't help but smile. She'd known Rob and his husband, Andy, for as long as she'd been coming to the island.

Anna could remember Rob and Andy buying the old, run-down restaurant and had watched over the years as they transformed The Water's Edge into a bustling bar and restaurant, popular with locals and tourists alike.

'There you go, Susie.' He placed a coffee in front of Anna and took the seat opposite. 'Any further forward today?'

'No. There must be something I'm missing, but I don't know where else to look. I took photos today of The Old

Lodge, but there was someone there. A man, just walking around the outside, but he had paperwork in his hand. He wasn't happy to see me, at all, and started shouting. When I turned to leave, he followed, then chased when I ran.'

'That's odd.' A concerned frown wrinkled his forehead.

'I know. I managed to get a few photos of him just before he saw me, so I'm hoping I've managed to snap a clear shot of his face.'

'Okay, give us a shout when you have them up. You know we're here if you need us, Susie, but be careful, please.' Rob rose from his seat to deal with the swelling queue at the bar.

Anna gave him a cheeky grin. For as long as she could remember, he had called her *Susie*. He knew she hated it, and she knew he did it purely to wind her up. Her real name was Susanna, but everyone, apart from Rob, called her *Anna*. Even her own mother couldn't bear to hear her called *Susanna*, and Anna had never understood why she was given a name her mother had disliked so much. But that was just one of the many mysteries that now surrounded her mother.

Soaking in the warmth from the fire, Anna waited as her images uploaded from her camera to her laptop. The Wi-Fi was always a little slower on the island, but that just reflected island life. Everything was calmer; the people were calmer. And she always struggled to get back into the pace of things when she returned to Edinburgh.

This winter was different though. This winter she was staying on in her cottage on the island. The mystery of her mother's letter far more alluring than central heating and a short walk to a supermarket, no matter the weather.

'You hungry yet, Susie?' Rob whispered, hurrying past with two hot plates to deliver to a neighbouring table. 'Andy's testing a new recipe. If you fancy being a guinea pig, it's on the house?' he finished as he hurried back to the bar.

'Oh, yes please. Surprise me.'

3

The uploads complete, Anna squinted as she zoomed in on the first photograph. But clicking from image to image, she couldn't quite make out the stranger's face. 'Come on, come on. Look up. Look up.' she muttered, her finger clicking on.

The stranger appeared to be studying the front of the lodge, the crest above the door, perhaps. But Anna continued flicking through the images, one by one, until, with her final click, a clean shot of the stranger's face. He was looking straight at the camera and Anna could feel her shoulders rise with the same panic she'd felt earlier.

'Here you are. You know the drill. An honest review for a free dinner,' Andy joked, placing on the table a tantalising plate of chicken and bacon with a sundried tomato cream sauce, a medley of roasted vegetables, and Anna's favourite fries.

'Oh, thank you. That smells delicious,' she said, going straight for the fries.

'Rob tells me you'd no luck today.'

'No, but I spotted this man at the lodge. He saw me taking photos and wasn't best pleased. Do you know him?' she asked, dipping fries into Andy's delicious sauce.

'No, never seen him before.' Andy leaned in for a closer look. 'You got a sec, Rob?'

Rob finished clearing a neighbouring table and came over.

'You recognise this guy?'

'Nope. He's certainly not local.'

'Na, too well-dressed. A city type, maybe.'

Anna inadvertently zoned out as they carried on their conversation. Andy's delicious cooking, the coal fire, and the company of the two men – the nearest thing to family she had – was just the tonic she'd needed. She'd reluctantly stopped short of ordering a glass of wine; that would have meant a taxi home.

'We'll keep our eyes peeled, love. Just you eat up.' Andy smiled, rubbing the evening's special off the board.

. . .

4

Anna had finished her dinner and had told Andy how wonderful a cook he was. Sipping slowly at another coffee, she decided to click through her photographs one more time. She zoomed in on the stranger's paperwork. It appeared to be just a single sheet of A4 paper, but she was disappointed to find its contents illegible.

She was just taking her final sip when the door opened. A man, early-thirties, dressed as though he was more suited to a city office than a restaurant in a small island town, walked in. Anna turned to face the fire and sat stock-still while he had a good look around before taking his place in the queue at the bar.

Returning her focus to her laptop, she clicked through the photographs until she found the clear image of the man she'd encountered earlier.

She slammed the lid shut and rammed the laptop into her rucksack. Rob looked up just in time to see her tying herself in knots as she tried, and failed, to put on her fleece and coat *and* pick up her camera and rucksack all in one swift movement.

'Hey, Su—'

He stopped, clocking the man at the bar. 'Can I help you?'

'Yeah, I don't suppose you know who owns the old jeep parked across the road?'

'Who's asking?' Rob stiffened.

'Just curious. A pint of IPA, please.'

CHAPTER TWO

Anna snuggled under a blanket on her sofa and poured herself a glass of wine. The stranger having messed with her evening meant it was too late to light the wood burner and too early to go to bed. Pulling the blanket further towards her chin, she cursed him as she sipped her wine.

Anna would often wait until the restaurant was closing, help tidy up, and sit and chat with the only two constants in her life. And, undoubtedly, she could have done with their company tonight.

Rob and Andy were both in their early fifties and were like fathers to her. After her mother had died, they were all she'd had, and as a result, she'd found herself spending more and more time on the island.

Rob and Andy were with Anna at her mother's bedside when she passed away peacefully. It was coming up to eight years ago, but Anna still felt as though it were yesterday.

She hadn't long turned twenty-three and was in her final year at Edinburgh University when her mother's health had rapidly deteriorated. And in what was to be her last conversation with her mother, Anna had promised she would finish her degree.

'That money came from a good heart. Promise me, promise me you'll finish your degree and find your way in the world,' her mother had pleaded.

Anna had nodded through her tears. It was the only thing she could do for her mother. She couldn't save her. She couldn't make her better. But she could fulfil her promise.

In the months that followed her mother's death, Anna still had her dissertation to complete, and she'd only managed that with the love and support she'd received from both Rob and Andy. Rob had dropped everything and remained in Edinburgh to be with her, while Andy returned to the island to keep the restaurant running. But he had called her regularly, and Anna knew it had broken his heart not to be with her.

Rob was there for her every morning when she left for the university library and every evening when she returned home. He made sure she ate properly and socialised with friends.

Both he and Andy were there for her graduation, and although bittersweet, it was a day that held happy memories for Anna. It was the day she had fulfilled her promise to her mother. And it had given her a sense of making her mother proud.

Anna reached for the wooden box that sat, pride of place, on her coffee table. She placed it on her lap, allowing her fingers to follow the ornate carvings, just as they had done so many times before. It was old, the markings worn, but it had a smell that took her back to her childhood. A smell she had been unable to place.

It wasn't until well after graduation that Anna had mustered the courage needed to look through and sort out her mother's belongings. She'd found the thought of going into her mother's bedroom too difficult. But, eventually, enough time had passed, and she'd spent a weekend in tears, with cuddles from Rob, as they sorted through the belongings together. That was when she had found the wooden box.

It had been tucked at the back of a deep drawer, alongside an old painting wrapped in multiple layers of bubble wrap. Rob had been uncharacteristically lost for words when Anna had removed the wrapping to reveal an oil paint landscape. 'Wow. That looks like an original. That might be worth a fair bit, Susie!' he'd said.

Anna could remember them squinting to read the signature, but given it was mostly hidden by the sealed frame, the artist had remained a mystery.

Anna had no idea how her mother had come to have something so exquisite and potentially expensive. But she had known she must have had a good reason for keeping it hidden away, especially given the amount of artwork her mother had managed to cram onto the walls of their flat over the years. Anna had wondered if her father had given it to her as a gift, or maybe an old boyfriend, and that was why her mother had chosen not to hang it with the others.

There'd not been as much money left in the bank as Anna would have expected. A couple of thousand pounds worth of savings, boosted by a life insurance policy. But where was the rest?

Her mother had bought their upmarket Stockbridge flat. It was beautiful. Three bedrooms, in a sought-after area of Edinburgh. She'd taken them on foreign holidays. They'd become accustomed to a certain standard of living. But had all of this taken a toll on her mother's savings?

Using money from the life insurance policy, Anna had set up her photography business. Despite the heartache of losing her mother, she knew she had a lot to be grateful for. She worked mostly freelance but had secured a regular spot writing for a monthly magazine, and her landscapes of the Scottish Highlands and Islands were always in demand. She supplied a number of galleries both on the mainland and throughout the islands and was slowly building her reputation, while her online shop had built her a customer base, particularly in the USA and Australia.

It was her job that allowed her to spend so much time on the island. She could work anywhere; she just had to make sure her monthly article was submitted on time. With her income from the magazine and galleries, alongside what was left from her mother's life insurance policy, Anna eventually had enough money to put down a deposit on her small, one-bedroom island cottage.

She knew she could never part with her mother's Edinburgh flat. It had been her childhood home, and it was handy to have a place to stay when she had to return to the city. But Skye was her sanctuary. Whether it was therapy, her need to be away from the pain of losing her mother, or just her love for the island, she could never quite decide. All she knew was she kept staying longer and longer with each visit.

She had originally spent the summer months on the island. Then it became summer through to autumn. This year she had come up in time for spring, and now, as winter snuck in, she felt this was the time and place to cope with the mystery of her mother's wooden box. She was staying on indefinitely.

Just about big enough to hold a pair of shoes, the box reeked of age and history. And she sensed, if it could speak, it would certainly have stories to tell.

Knowing its contents inside out, she instinctively opened the lid. There was the black-and-white photograph set in the antique silver frame that had caused her the most anguish. The middle-aged couple looked pleasant, happy, and confident, but Anna found their anonymity unsettling. And there was the letter.

* * *

In early January, when she'd returned to Edinburgh for a few weeks after spending Christmas and New Year with Rob and Andy, she'd gone through her mother's possessions again.

She missed her mother terribly and needed the comfort of her belongings. Sitting on her mother's bed with a cup of tea in one hand, surrounded by tear-soaked tissues, she spotted a bulge in the back of the frame. As she removed the rear casing, another smaller photograph, and a piece of paper folded several times, fell onto her lap.

The photograph was of a large house. Anna recognised it instantly. The Old Lodge, which sat a few miles south of Dunvegan, nestled about halfway up a rolling hill, its entrance opposite the dirt track that led to Lochside.

It was an area Anna knew well. She would often stop to photograph the sea loch from the jetty at Lochside when travelling between her cottage in Staffin and the galleries she delivered to on the western side of the island. And if Abigail was at home, they'd sit and enjoy a coffee as they looked out at the views and would catch up on each other's news.

She set the photograph of The Old Lodge aside and carefully unwrapped the paper, finding her mother's handwriting.

My darling Anna,

If you have found this letter then I am most certainly no longer with you. There are things you need to know, things I should have told you a long time ago. Please believe me when I say I tried, but I could never quite find the words. We were so happy, you and I, and I didn't want you to be disappointed in me, to think less of me, but to keep the truth from you forever would be unfair.

Do you remember our little adventures to Skye? The memories we made there were priceless to me, my darling, but the wonderful Isle of Skye holds so much more for you. I have lied to you, Anna, but I didn't know what else to do. When I told you your grandparents were dead, well, that wasn't true, at least not at the time of writing. Your grandparents, my parents, are still very much alive and living on the island.

My father and I had never gotten along; I wasn't what he envisaged. I didn't want to take over the family croft. I wanted to be free, to live my small valuable life my way. I wanted to paint the world. I wanted to try and make my living through my art and make a name for myself if I could.

The final straw had been your father. My father didn't approve of him. We had only been together a few months when I fell pregnant, and I knew our relationship would never last. He was the son of my father's rival. It wasn't so much my pregnancy that angered my father, but the fear of this other family becoming involved with ours. He feared for his business and for his land. And I'm ashamed to say, I went out of my way to encourage his fear.

I was eventually sent off the island and away from your father. It broke my mother's heart, but she knew it would be better for me in the long run. She knew that my leaving could open opportunities for me as an artist, something I wrongly assumed my father would have made difficult for me had I stayed.

Looking back, I didn't make life easy for your grandfather. I antagonised him. And, if I'm truly honest, it was far simpler to stay angry at him than to swallow my pride and make amends.

My mother had a friend in Edinburgh, and the day I left the island, she made me promise that I would go straight to the city. She told me her friend would be waiting for me.

My mother and I would send messages back and forth to each other through her friend. It was my mother, your grandmother, who paid the mortgage on our home until it was paid off. My father thought it was just another of her investments, but my mother gave us a roof over our heads, and now it belongs to you.

My mother always knew when we were travelling to the island, and she would be there, somewhere in the distance, watching us. But she would never make contact. No matter how much I begged. She stayed loyal to my father. Deep down, I think she feared the trouble I might cause if she allowed herself to reopen old wounds. But I had learned my lesson. It's why

I devoted my life to ensuring I became a better person and a mother you could be proud of. My regret is that my parents never got to know the person I became.

Do you remember the days when we would sit by the sea, and I would joke that the sound of the waves made me sad? Well, those were the days that I'd spotted her, your grandmother, watching us from across the street or through a shop window. Her eyes were always on you. She loved you as though she saw you every day, and it was her biggest heartache that she had been denied you.

Be strong, my darling daughter. Live life the way you always have, with courage and passion. Finish your degree. Find your way in the world and a happiness that is truly yours. Do not change who you are for anyone, and above all, love, as I will love you, always.

Mum x

* * *

Anna sobbed, just as she always did when she read her mother's letter. But she knew the time had come for her to start a little digging into her mother's family and her life growing up on the island.

She had often wondered about the couple in the photograph. Were they her mother's parents, her grandparents? She assumed so. But given the years that had passed since her mother's death, Anna knew she couldn't just presume they would still be alive. There was also no mention in the letter of whether her mother had siblings. If her mother had been an only child, Anna knew it was highly possible there would be no family left to find.

Anna wasn't sure how she felt about her grandparents. She knew she didn't want to meet them, especially her grandfather, given the way he had treated her mother. But the ability to create a family tree, to know a little about where she came from, would be a comfort in her lonely world.

She had just submitted her monthly article to the magazine, meaning she had a couple of weeks before she needed to start putting together the next, and she already had an idea for the subject matter.

The first thing Anna had hoped to discover was what part The Old Lodge had played in her mother's life. And why her mother had taken the trouble to include the photograph with her letter.

This was a question that had been troubling Anna from the moment she had first discovered the photograph. And it was why she had been photographing The Old Lodge that morning, before she had been chased off by the stranger.

Feeling indignant, most probably from the wine, Anna decided it was time to ignite some courage. She would return to the lodge in the morning and finish what she had started.

CHAPTER THREE

Parking in the same spot as the previous day, Anna grabbed her camera and retraced her steps towards The Old Lodge. Reaching the grass verge that separated the dirt track from the now overgrown driveway, Anna checked for any sign of the mysterious stranger.

The imposing building stood at an angle. Its secretive windows overlooked the receding hill and the North Atlantic in the distance, as the winter winds howled around its weathered exterior.

Edging ever closer, Anna clicked her camera repeatedly. Photography was her way of documenting the building, her way of taking notes. Zooming in, she clicked on every crevice, the decorative stone around the main door, and the windows that alluded to many rooms.

But it was all faded grandeur now. Dark, dismal, and empty. Grass had encroached where planted beds had once fought with the Scottish weather for survival. But, to Anna, the building still retained an air of beauty. Its presence — its elegance — was calming.

Her camera continued to click as she edged past the front

door towards the farthest side of the lodge. Clicking with every step. Documenting everything from the eroded crest above the front door to the cracked chimney pots.

Click, click, click; a melodic noise she loved. Anna could never take too many photographs. To her, each was different. The angle may have changed only slightly, but that meant the light and the dimensions of the building would be completely different.

The soothing clicks continued, her feet grappling for balance as she stumbled over the uneven ground and eroded gravel that now surrounded the lodge. She edged closer, towards the building and into a past she could only imagine. Her camera never leaving her eye. Lost in the moment. Lost in the history and the contours of a building that had insisted on invading her thoughts from the moment she had discovered the photograph with her mother's letter.

But a frantic knocking on glass broke her concentration. Its persistence guided her towards the upper floor. A face, looking out, mouthed to her to stay where she was before disappearing into the darkness of the lodge.

Stomach lurching. Fear spreading through her body like tentacles. Anna's first reaction was to stay rooted to the spot. But she was sure the lodge had been abandoned, that no one lived there, and she had seen no one in all the time she'd been photographing it. Managing to coax herself into running, she headed towards her jeep.

She was just approaching the grass verge when she heard a voice shouting to her to stop. Turning, she saw the man from yesterday. He was running towards her, sheet of paper in one hand, while the other urged her to stop.

But with no other soul in sight, Anna continued to run, the vast landscape stretching for miles with only sheep and a splattering of trees for company. On reaching the safety of her jeep, she jumped in and sped down the hill in yet another cloud of dust, just as she had done the previous day.

Turning onto the main road, she slowed down, keeping pace with the traffic in front. But she wanted home. She wanted to feel safe in her cottage, with the door locked.

Her heart still pounded as she crossed the island to Portree before heading north to Staffin.

Almost home, she turned off to the right, onto a dirt track. Her cottage sat just a quarter of a mile from the main road that snaked through the village, but each time she turned onto her track, she felt she was in her own little bubble. This was her patch of the island.

Normally, Anna would abandon her jeep at her front door. But this time, she continued around to the back of her cottage, parking out of sight of the main road.

The idyllic village of Staffin lay scattered either side of the main road north from Portree, so Anna knew there was every chance the lodge's mysterious visitor could drive by at any time, and her jeep didn't exactly blend in.

Anna unlocked her front door and picked up her mail. There was a *Sorry We Missed You* card telling her a package had been left behind her cottage. It was a much-anticipated fresh supply of mounts she'd ordered from a new supplier.

Having spent the last few weeks working on a new sequence of prints, Anna was now ready to mount them. A small number would also be framed, and her plan was to deliver them to the various galleries over the next couple of weeks. Most were to be delivered to the mainland as many of the smaller galleries on the island had already closed for the winter months.

* * *

ANNA'S COTTAGE HAD BEEN NEWLY RENOVATED WHEN SHE'D FIRST come to view it. Still nervous at the thought of a mortgage, she'd been back and forth, viewing it several times before finally being brave enough to sign on the dotted line.

It was small and affordable, but homely, and it was hers. The front door led straight into her living room-cum-kitchen, which had been tastefully separated by a breakfast bar. She had fallen in love with the Belfast sink, wood burner, and contemporary décor the cottage had received during its renovation, and she'd recently made space for her mother's old desk at the front-facing window. She was looking forward to bringing it up from Edinburgh when she was next back in the city as she found the views of the Trotternish Ridge with the Quiraing in the distance inspiring, no matter the weather. She knew it would be the ideal set up for writing the magazine articles that accompanied her photography.

A narrow hallway at the front of the cottage led off to the right, with a small but elegantly finished bathroom nestled between the kitchen and the bedroom positioned neatly at the opposite end of the cottage. The bedroom wasn't a massive room due to the newly built-in wardrobes, but there was still room for a double bed and a couple of chests of drawers.

The *pièce de résistance* for Anna was the spiral staircase that led from the bedroom to the converted loft. There wasn't much headroom, but Anna loved it. She had turned it into her studio. With her PC and printer set up at one end, she could edit, print, mount, and frame her photographs in preparation for delivery to the various galleries, shops, and tourist attractions she had managed to build relationships with over the years. She loved how the light from the Velux windows splayed across her images in varying and dramatic forms, depending on the Scottish weather.

Anna pulled her camera from her rucksack and began uploading the pictures she had taken earlier to her PC, but the gurgling from her stomach reminded her it was lunchtime.

An involuntary sigh escaped as she opened her fridge.

17

Having been preoccupied with the lodge in recent days, she hadn't been near a supermarket. And deciding a trip to Portree was in order later that afternoon, she put two slices of bread in the toaster. Toast and jam being her only option!

Taking her uninspiring lunch up to her converted loft, Anna began looking through the photographs. Crunching through the toast she had cheered up with a mug of hot chocolate, Anna clicked from one photo to the next. She was pleasantly surprised to see The Old Lodge wasn't nearly as dilapidated as she had initially thought. The windows were filthy, their frames desperately in need of a lick of paint, and a couple of chimney pots needed repaired. But apart from that, the lodge was looking structurally sound. The overgrown garden and driveway had added to the lodge's overall dilapidated appearance, Anna decided, continuing to click through the remaining images. Settling on the crest above the front door, she squinted, trying to make out the worn etchings in the stone, but it was too faint. Hugging her mug between her hands, she contemplated her next move. A visit to Portree was in order.

Resisting the temptation to drive towards The Water's Edge, Anna continued to Dunvegan Road and the archive centre.

Nestled beside the library and Portree High School, the Skye and Lochalsh Archive Centre was a building Anna had driven past often but never had the need to visit. The thought of learning more about the lodge and its possible connection to her past meant Anna was sure she was about to unearth all the information she craved.

She met the archivist, a pleasant middle-aged lady, and gave her the address to The Old Lodge. The archivist smiled at the mere mention of the building. A place she must know well, Anna decided, as the archivist continued to make light conversation while searching for old newspaper articles and records held for the lodge.

'So, are you from the island or researching for a project? You don't sound local?'

'A bit of both. My mum came from Skye, but she left when she was pregnant with me. I grew up in Edinburgh. I've bought a cottage here, though.' Anna tailed off, realising that in the last year most of her time had been spent on the island. She hadn't thought about Edinburgh as *home* in months. 'Anyway,' she continued, 'I'm just curious about The Old Lodge. I drive past it all the time and I'm a photographer, so the building and its history appeals to me. I thought I might do a piece on it for a magazine I write for.'

'Oh, that sounds exciting,' the older woman gushed. 'And what was your mother's name? I might know her. We're probably about the same age?'

'Helena MacLeod.'

The archivist paused. Her fingers, that only moments before had expertly rifled through records and tapped keyboards, became still. She turned to Anna. 'And your name?'

'Susanna, but everyone calls me Anna.'

The archivist became flustered. Not another word was uttered while she continued her search.

After what felt an eternity, the archivist returned her attention to Anna.

'Here's some things to get you started. I don't want to bombard you with information, not today.' She continued, giving Anna an awkward sideways glance. 'This will be enough for you to get your head around for now, I'm sure. There's more online, but we can get to that another time.'

'Okay, thank you,' Anna replied, following the archivist into the search room.

'I'll be at the desk if you need me. I'm local, born and brought up here, so can help if you need to chat anything over.

My name's Cristine, but everyone calls me Crissie.' She emptied her laden arms and signalled for Anna to sit.

Thanking Crissie, Anna took her seat. The pile was topped by a newspaper. The Old Lodge had been that day's front-page news, and its picture showed the lodge in all its grandeur.

The driveway, a dirt track that gave way to sculpted gravel, was as neat and elegant as Anna had imagined, while the garden had been kept as tidy as the island weather and barren landscape would allow.

An old but fancy car was parked at the side of the lodge, and as is the norm throughout the island, sheep were grazing on the hillside and the rugged grounds surrounding the lodge. The headline read: 'Maren Bay House to open its door to the public.'

Maren Bay House! Anna had only ever known it as The Old Lodge. Even the ageing, rickety wooden sign at the bottom of the dirt track was labelled: *The Old Lodge*. But, to Anna, this new information gave the building a much grander presence and instant history. Squinting, she began to read the faint text. 'Iain MacLeod to open his doors to those summering on Skye.'

Acknowledging that Iain MacLeod must have been an important figure on the island to have received a front-page spread that spilled over onto the following page, Anna read on. But she was disappointed there was nothing of substance to help her in the article.

Turning her attention back to the bundle Crissie had given her, Anna began working her way through the rest of the articles, photographs, and notes.

Iain MacLeod was a prominent man on the island, that was obvious, but there was nothing telling her about what he did, how he came to own such a grand house, or who his family were.

There were many MacLeods on the island. Anna had always known that – she was one of them. Articles and records confirmed that Dunvegan Castle belonged to MacLeods, but there was nothing linking the lodge to them or the castle.

Rising from her seat, she went to find Crissie.

'Any good?'

'Yes, it was lovely to see the old photographs and the building looking so well kept, but there was nothing about the family, what they did or who they were, apart from naming Iain MacLeod. Do you hold any information on them, a family tree, maybe? Anything at all about who they were, what they did, their occupations, or how they came to own and live in the house?'

'Erm, I, eh…Just a minute.' Crissie wandered over to speak to a colleague – or, rather, whisper. Their hushed tones and glances were giving Anna an uneasy feeling, but she waited patiently.

'Can you come back tomorrow? I could take half an hour and sit with you. Go through the family in a bit more detail.'

'That would be great, but are you sure you have the time?'

'Yes, of course. Why don't you come in about two thirty? That way, I'll have cleared the decks a bit and I'll be able to sit with you for a while.'

Thanking Crissie, Anna wrapped herself in her coat and scarf before heading out into the winter chill.

Shivering from the island winds, Anna drove the short distance to the supermarket. Food shopping was more a chore than a pleasure for Anna. She tended to rush around throwing whatever she liked the look of into her trolley without giving much thought to what she would do with it, when she would eat it, or how she would cook it.

To Anna, it was about getting the shopping done and escaping the supermarket as quickly as possible. Today, though, her thoughts were on dinner. The toast and jam she'd had for lunch hadn't done much in the way of filling her up, and she fancied something extra tasty.

Having filled her trolley with much-needed essentials, Anna browsed the bung-in-the-oven section before finally deciding dinner would be a trip to The Water's Edge. Smiling contentedly at her decision, she cut her shopping trip short and finished via the ice cream and confectionery aisles before joining a small queue at the tills.

Ten minutes later, Anna was leaving with a plan in her head: home, shopping away, a couple of hours of photo editing, before heading to The Water's Edge for dinner and family time with Rob and Andy. The mere thought brought an involuntary smile to Anna's face.

With her thoughts lost in The Water's Edge menu, Anna was startled to notice a male figure leaning against her jeep. With one leg crossed in front of the other and his arms folded, the stranger cut a worrying figure.

'Please, don't run this time,' he begged.

Recognising him from the photographs she had taken at the lodge, Anna could feel her stomach lurch. But a quick check of the car park and, although not bustling, she was relieved to see they weren't alone.

'You're Anna, aren't you?'

Shocked that he knew her name, Anna remained silent.

'You haven't changed. You're older, but it's still you.'

'We've met?'

'No, but your photograph's always been in my mum's living room.'

'My photograph? Why, who are you?'

'I'm Ben Sutherland. Does my name mean anything to you?'

'No, should it?'

'I thought maybe you and your family would know me, know my family.'

Anna smirked. 'I don't know my own family, so there's not much chance I'll know yours.'

'But you've been up at the big house twice this week, at least.'

'I'm often there, but that doesn't mean I know you,' she retorted indignantly, at the same time becoming unsettled at him knowing her movements. 'What's The Old Lodge got to do with anything, anyway?'

'I don't know. I was hoping you'd tell me.'

Anna looked at him properly for the first time. He was similar in age to her, and on closer inspection, didn't look the type to abduct her. In fact, he looked quite harmless and totally out of place in his city clothes.

But she did notice that, while from a distance his clothes had given the impression he was a professional working for an upmarket city firm, they didn't look quite so impressive close up. He was trying too hard, she decided. 'Why do you think I can help?'

'Well, we're obviously connected somehow. I grew up with your picture on the mantelpiece, and we're both interested in the big house.'

It seemed Ben was getting unsettled, panicked, almost.

'We have to talk,' he said, raising his voice. 'We have to work out who we are and where we came from.'

'I know exactly who I am, thank you very much. I'm Anna, and I'm from Edinburgh.'

The winter wind bit at their faces, their cold breath intertwining as their conversation became more animated.

'Anna's short for Susanna, isn't it?'

'H-how do you know?'

'Because that's what my mum always calls you.'

'Who's your mum?'

'Maggie Sutherland. She lives in Aberdeen.'

Anna allowed the name *Maggie Sutherland* to penetrate the farthest reaches of her memories, thinking back to the conversations she'd had with her mother and the discoveries she'd made since her mother's death. She was aware of Ben stepping closer, eagerly – desperately, perhaps – searching her face for a flicker of recognition.

'Look, it's freezing out here,' he interrupted. 'Can we go somewhere and talk, please?'

Anna's thoughts turned to the ice cream lurking temptingly at the bottom of her shopping bags. 'Okay, but can we meet later? I'm heading to The Water's Edge tonight. Meet you there about seven thirty?'

'Okay, great, yes, thank you. See you then.'

Watching Ben drive off in the overly shiny car that had been parked next to hers, Anna thought about how flustered, yet relieved, he had become when she'd agreed to meet. Something was off, and although wary, she knew she had to listen to what he had to say if she was going to get to the bottom of why he was hanging around the lodge.

* * *

Driving out of Portree, Anna reflected on her conversation with Ben. Neither his nor his mother's name had meant anything to her. But then why would they? Her mother had never spoken of her family. She'd always insisted she had none. But, that apart, Anna was realising her mother had no reminders of family in their Edinburgh home. There were no family photos sitting out other than those of herself and Anna. And there were no heirlooms or childhood memories that Anna knew of, other than the old oil painting she had found alongside the wooden box. Which brought Anna to an alarming realisation: everything she knew about her extended family was written in that one letter from her mother.

Slowing to allow wandering sheep to clear from the road, Anna felt a wave of isolation wash over her, something she had never experienced before. She had felt lonely after her mother's death, but this was different. It was as though every living being in the world was interconnected in some way. Their families, friendships, and connections drawing them ever closer. Apart from her. She was alone, isolated in a vast universe.

Her university friends had drifted off in their varying directions after graduation, and apart from *liking* a few social media posts, and the odd message, her little world mostly consisted of Rob, Andy and her catchups with Abigail.

By the time she had abandoned her jeep in front of her cottage, tears were streaming down Anna's cheeks. And unloading her shopping and replenishing her fridge did little to console her. Knowing she wouldn't be able to concentrate on editing photographs or writing her article, she filled her Thermos mug with tea, wrapped up warm, and ventured out to seek the calmness of the island.

Fortunate in that her cottage had a slightly elevated view, Anna could see the Trotternish Ridge as it reached all the way to the Quiraing. With cottages dappled in the foreground, the land soon gave way to the vast, barren landscape that, combined with the rugged coastline, forged the island's beauty.

Sitting on the wooden bench she'd inherited with the cottage, Anna closed her eyes. Bleating sheep, squawking gulls, and the whoosh of the wind enveloped her as she sipped at her hot, comforting tea.

She revisited her conversation with Ben for the second time, and his words danced in her head, intermingling with her conversation with Crissie and the articles she'd read in the archive centre.

Nature's serenade, combined with her soothing tea, meant Anna was beginning to relax, making sense of her day and all she had discovered. Which led to the realisation that Crissie's comments now seemed a little odd: *I don't want to bombard you with information, not today,* and *This will be enough for you to get your head around for now.* Then there was the expression on Crissie's face when Anna had given her mother's name.

Apart from Rob and Andy, the few people she knew on the island knew her simply as *Anna*, her surname seldom relevant in day-to-day island life. There were the postmen, who although similar in age to her mother, would see no connection, given her mail had no reference to *Helena*.

Anna was also realising Crissie was right: she would have been a similar age to her mother, and therefore, there was every reason she could have known her. Suddenly, the thought of chatting with Ben appealed, and seven thirty couldn't come soon enough.

Her phone pinged. A message from Abigail.

Hi, we're in Portree, if you're about? Would love a quick chat. Could meet you in The Water's Edge? xx

Glancing at her phone – only 5.15 p.m. – Anna realised that if she were to go to The Water's Edge now, she could meet Abigail, have dinner, and enjoy the comforting company of Rob and Andy, all before Ben arrived.

And rushing to her bedroom, she winced as she caught sight of her tear-stained face. But a quick wash, fresh make-up, and her long hair brushed and pulled back into a ponytail, soon gave her the transformation she had hoped for.

She didn't resemble her mother in any way. Anna's blonde, poker-straight hair and watery blue eyes were in stark contrast to Helena's wavy brown locks and green eyes. They had shared the same sense of humour, though, and both had the ability to cheer the other up. A side of her mother that Anna had been missing the most in recent months.

CHAPTER FOUR

Walking into The Water's Edge, Anna spotted Abigail and Jamie at the bar. Rob was giving them both a hug and a few locals were out of their chairs shaking Jamie's hand and hugging Abigail.

By the time Anna had fought her way through the packed restaurant, Rob was showing them both to a table with enough chairs for the three of them. And by the time Anna shed her winter layers, Rob was back with three menus.

'Have you got time to join us for dinner?' Abigail asked, getting to her feet to give Anna a welcome hug.

'Eh, yeah, sure, as long as I'm not intruding.'

'Don't be daft. We were hoping you'd be free.'

'We were,' Jamie added, giving Anna a hug and handing her a menu.

'Okay, great.' Anna scanned her menu, grateful for the timing of their invite.

With Rob waiting on their table, there was no shortage of laughter as he brought them drinks and took their food orders.

'So, what's the occasion?' Anna teased. 'It's not like you two to be over this side of the island at this time of day.'

'Well, we do have some news,' Abigail announced, her eyes twinkling with excitement as she beamed her biggest smile.

'We do.' Jamie's grin mirrored Abigail's.

'What?' The grinning was infectious. 'What's your news?'

Abigail slunk her hand in front of Anna. A solitaire stood proud with diamonds set into a gold band that shimmered and sparkled under the glow of the lights. Hugs and toasts all round as Anna congratulated her friends, thoroughly delighted for them both. After all they had been through – Anna's heart was bursting with love and excitement for them, while Abigail and Jamie looked the epitome of happiness.

Anna raised her glass. 'To the most wonderful couple I know. Congratulations.'

And after the clinking of glasses had subsided, she added, 'So, tell me all about it, Jamie. How and where did you propose?'

'Where else?' he gushed, looking at Abigail. 'On our jetty—'

'As the sun was setting,' Abigail interrupted. 'The sky was magical. The loch was relatively calm, for the time of year.' She chuckled. 'It was just us. It was perfect.'

'I'm so happy for you both.' Anna was thoroughly excited for them and revelled in hearing some good news, for a change. 'Have you made any plans yet?'

'Not yet. I'll get this next book launch out of the way and then we'll start making plans. I've already told Joanna that as soon as we have a date set, we'll be blocking out the calendar, and she'd better behave.'

'Good luck there.' Anna laughed. 'And your parents, Jamie? They must be thrilled.'

'That's putting it mildly.'

BY THE TIME THEY HAD FINISHED DINNER, ANNA WAS FEELING back to her old self. The company of two friends had done her the world of good, and her delight for Abigail and Jamie had cheered her up after a strange couple of days.

Abigail and Jamie were just hugging Anna goodbye when Ben walked into the restaurant. Aware of Rob throwing her a *please be wary* glance, she smiled at Ben as he took the seat beside her.

'Thanks for meeting me, Anna. I was worried you'd had second thoughts.'

'Well, it turns out I have a whole list of questions for you too.'

'Such as?'

'Such as why is my photograph on a mantelpiece in Aberdeen?'

'My mum's from Skye.'

'That doesn't exactly answer my question.'

'She won't tell me. She just maintains that you deserve to have your picture out and that what happened wasn't fair, given all that had gone on.'

Anna leaned forward. 'What do you mean, *all that had gone on*?'

'I'm sorry, I don't know. When I saw you at the big house the other day, I just presumed you'd be able to answer all *my* questions.'

'Okay, so, why were you at The Old Lodge and how did you manage to get inside?'

'Key.'

'Key? You have a key?'

'Yes. Well, kind of.'

'Kind of?'

'It's my mum's, from years ago. I've unofficially borrowed it. Look, I think I should get us both a drink. There's obviously lots we need to talk about.' He picked up Anna's empty glass. 'Same again?'

Nodding, she watched Ben approach the bar. And although

29

he appeared to be just as oblivious to his past as she was to hers, Anna knew she had to get to the bottom of why her photograph was sitting on a mantelpiece in Aberdeen.

'Were our mums sisters?' Her words were out before Ben had a chance to retake his seat.

'What?'

'Were our mums sisters?'

'I-I've no idea. N-no, my mum's an only one.'

'As far as you know.'

'Well, yes, but why would she lie about that?'

'Maybe she isn't. I'm just trying to find the connection.'

Noticing Ben's expression, Anna couldn't help but feel he was holding back, that he perhaps knew more than he was letting on.

'Okay, let's start over,' he suggested nervously, sipping his pint. 'My mum has lived in Aberdeen since she married my dad, but they divorced when I was young and she went back to her maiden name, Sutherland.'

'Well, they're not sisters then because my surname's MacLeod. My mum was a MacLeod.'

'But is that not her married name?'

'She was never married. She didn't stay with my dad. My mum left the island before I was born.'

'So…So you're a MacLeod?'

'Yes.'

Ben fell silent.

'What difference does my surname make? What are you not telling me?'

'Nothing.' Another nervous sip of his pint. 'I just didn't realise your mum was a MacLeod, that's all.' Stiffening, he regained his composure. 'Do you think your dad would know who my mum is? Or your mum, maybe? I have a picture?'

'I have no idea who my dad is – my mum never told me –

and looking back, I never really needed to know.' Anna shrugged.

'And your mum?'

Slumping back in her chair, Anna had discovered that if she said it quickly and with purpose, she could say what needed to be said without becoming a blubbering wreck. 'My mum passed away, quite a few years ago now.'

'Oh, Anna, I'm so sorry, I-I really am. My mum obviously doesn't know. Does that mean you're on your own?'

Anna didn't respond. Instead, she watched as Ben relaxed, the nervous, timid city gent disappearing before her eyes. He shuffled closer, seeming desperate to hear all she had to say.

Before she knew it, she had blurted out her entire life story. She may have come from a single parent family, but until her mother had fallen ill, Anna's upbringing had been happy, content, and full of wonderful memories. She had never felt that anyone or anything had been missing from her life.

In return, Ben told Anna about his childhood in Aberdeen. It hadn't been as happy as Anna's – he didn't have happy memories of his dad and preferred not to go into that too much – but she could tell he and his mum were close.

'Why don't you just ask your mum about the lodge, the island, and her life here?'

'She refuses to talk about it, point blank,' he replied, his eyes scanning the room.

'But why?'

He shrugged his shoulders. 'I've no idea.'

'So, what does she think of you coming here?'

'I haven't told her.'

He looked anywhere but at Anna.

'You haven't! But why?'

'I'm away a lot—with work,' he added nervously. 'She won't think anything of it. I've taken a couple of weeks' holiday. I'm staying in a guest house here in Portree.'

'And you have a key.' Her eyes widened. 'Can I see inside the lodge, please?'

'Yeah, sure. We can go tomorrow.'

She smiled and sipped her drink. The thought of gaining access to The Old Lodge was such an exciting prospect.

'Oh,' she blurted out. 'I've arranged to visit the archive centre tomorrow afternoon at two thirty.' And as she went on to tell Ben about her earlier visit and the reaction her mother's name had received from the archivist, Anna could feel the mysteries surrounding the lodge and her mother thickening. The words fell seamlessly from her lips, yet she was convinced they would find all the answers to their questions inside the lodge.

'Well, it sounds as though the archive centre might be helpful for both of us. What if we meet at the lodge, as you call it, about ten? We can reflect on what we discover over lunch and then head to the archive centre afterwards?'

'Actually, it's *Maren Bay House*, to give it its Sunday name.'

'Maren Bay House?'

Now it seemed to be Ben's turn to have his interest piqued. Anna was quick to spot the flicker of recognition in his eyes. 'You've heard of it?'

'Yes, eh, yeah,' he said, his eyes avoiding Anna's.

'Well?' she prompted.

'Oh, I-I remember my dad shouting about it when I was young. Yeah, he used to say it was more trouble than it was worth. I remember asking my mum about it, but she always said there was nothing to be gained from digging up the past.'

'So, if it was only ever a name to you, how did you know about the building here on Skye? Why were you at the lodge?'

'B-because, because there are pictures of it in albums,' Ben replied, momentarily losing his composure. 'They're from before my parents were married and going back a few genera-tions. I'd just wondered if it was still here. I'm doing the family tree, trying to trace family since ours seems to be so thin on the ground, and I thought if I could find the building, it might be a good place to start. I knew it was near Dunvegan, and I just drove there and showed the picture to a couple of locals, and they gave me directions. I found it the same day I arrived.'

'It seems to me like you're taking a risk. I mean, won't your mum be angry with you for doing this?'

Ben's composure slipped once again.

CHAPTER FIVE

Anna had barely slept. The excitement at seeing inside the lodge kept her awake for much of the night before eventually invading her dreams.

She'd arrived at the lodge well before ten and was photographing the surrounding scenery and the sheep that, ambivalent to her presence, had ventured close enough for her to snap a few opportune close-ups, when Ben arrived.

'Hey.'

She took her eye from the lens. He was striding towards her gripping the familiar, but now crumpled, sheet of paper in hand.

'Good grief,' she said, 'What have you got there?'

'Oh, nothing really.' He shrugged. 'Just thought I'd take some notes while we were here.'

She followed as he led the way, the excitement at finally seeing inside the lodge trembling through her body. He put the key in the lock. The scratching sound followed by a clunk as the old lock sprang into action seemed fitting, given the building's appearance.

Anna's legs powered her first few excited strides. Once

inside, however, they came to an abrupt halt as the faint aroma teasing her nostrils brought her mother's wooden box to the forefront of her mind.

Her heart pounding, she absorbed the splendour of her surroundings. The entrance hall was vast. A sweeping staircase floated off to her right and dominated the spacious hallway, a dark, wooden handrail snaking towards the first floor. Her eyes followed as the imposing handrail levelled off, allowing a glimpse of floral wallpaper that Anna could only hope had been stylish in its time.

Her attention returned to the ground floor, following the curving banister as it led down to the open hallway, culminating in a dramatic circular stop.

To the side, magnificent, old wooden panelling rose from floor to ceiling before seamlessly circling back on itself to create an impressive reception area.

'It's-it's been a hotel!' Announced Anna.

'Yeah, you didn't know?'

'There was something in a newspaper article in the archive centre, but I thought it had just been for a summer back in the seventies.'

With her hand gliding along the top of the perfectly polished reception area, Anna worked her way around until she was behind the reception desk. The bespoke shelving and built-in drawers still slid open and closed with ease. Each drawer divulging its own secrets of years gone by. Notebooks, pens, files, and folders that looked as though they had been used just yesterday sat neatly in position. It was as though the receptionist was merely on a coffee break and would return at any moment.

A slimmer top drawer slid open to reveal a tray made in the same wood, with sections numbered from one to twelve, each slot holding a key. Room keys, Anna presumed, her gaze rising once again to the splash of flamboyant wallpaper still teasing her from above.

'Come on, I'll show you around. The rooms aren't locked, so you can leave the keys.' Ben nodded towards a small door behind her, marked *Private*. Made in matching wood, it led them from behind the reception desk, beneath the staircase, to a surprisingly sprawling room.

'I'm presuming this was the owner's private quarters. It's more homely and less extravagant than the rest of the rooms,' Ben commented, standing aside to allow Anna to enter first.

There was silence, other than the clicking of her camera, as she absorbed the room through her lens. Stretching out in front of them, a bed, probably king-sized, dominated the farthest end of the room, while Anna and Ben found themselves standing in what was set out as a lounge area. A sofa, coffee table, and bookshelves laden with books stood out against pale painted walls creating the illusion of space, as though its occupants had an entire wing of the ground floor to themselves.

'Follow me,' Ben strode towards the farthest end of the room. Three doors in the same opulent wood as the staircase and panelling in the reception area led off to the right.

Stopping for a moment, disorientated, Anna circled the room. 'But…where do they go?'

'They're facing the front of the building. The one on the left is a bathroom,' Ben said. 'And there, in the middle, that's a big walk-in wardrobe.'

'And the one on the right?'

'Ah, wait till you see this. It's my favourite room in the building. Again, it's less grand than the rest of the place, but it's full of personal treasures. If you look, there's no other doorway in, so it feels almost like a secret room.'

'Wait, personal treasures?' A shiver tingled her spine. 'Does someone still live here?'

'No-no, but it does appear to have been abandoned. There's no food or clothing, but everything else has just been left. It's very odd, eerie in some rooms. There's an old guy living in the cottage further up the hill. He told me no one lives here, and he knows I've been looking around. It's fine.' He opened the door on the right and gestured to Anna to lead the way.

As she entered the cosy room, Anna tried to fathom why on earth someone would just up and leave The Old Lodge and all its contents behind. The room was a little smaller than she had expected, given the size of the lodge from outside, although the furnishing and cluttered walls possibly added to the feel. A small window held views out to the side. Grazing sheep scattered undisturbed across the undulating hillside.

'It reminds me of a snug.' Ben's voice broke into her thoughts. 'I think this is where the owners came to relax. What do you think?'

But Anna hadn't heard him.

Breathing in the familiar aroma, she had become light-headed. And as she struggled to untangle her emotions, the contents of her mother's wooden box leaped to the fore once again. Panic rising, she realised The Old Lodge was soon to mean more to her than just a fascination for the exterior.

Her breathing became laboured. Her heart racing, she gripped the door frame as a thunderous booming in her chest echoed in her ears. She looked from the window to the furniture laden with trinkets. How could she calm herself down? She needed to focus on the room, not how she was feeling. She needed to breathe.

Her strategy worked until she diverted her attention to the facing wall. Her legs were limp, motionless, while somersaults reduced her stomach to tangled knots. Her heart racing. Her body trembling, shivering, before giving way to nervous chills. Words choking in her throat.

Transported back in time, she was a little girl, sitting at the kitchen table, drawing, painting, colouring while her mother sat by her easel at the window. Anna was transfixed in the moment.

Her mother alive, laughing, chatting, but always keeping a keen eye on the Edinburgh skyline as she painted her latest project.

As Anna's eyes skimmed the cluttered walls, the beating in her chest grew louder, faster. Her breathing erratic; her body shaking involuntarily.

'Anna, what's wrong?'

Silence.

'Anna, Anna?'

She was rooted to the spot, lost in a whirlwind of emotions as her eyes drank in the countless paintings that covered every spare inch of the walls, reminiscent of a patchwork quilt.

Views of her childhood home lay before her. The park, open only to the residents of St Bernard's Crescent. The distant skyline that was evident only from the upper floor of their sprawling maisonette flat, in the building that had protected her entire existence. The splendid gardens.

Her eyes devoured oil paintings of the shared garden at the rear of her Edinburgh home, kept immaculate by Mr Hudson, a retired lawyer whose flat encompassed the ground and basement floor of their building. He had discovered late in life that gardening was his passion and had transformed the once neglected mess into a haven where Anna could play as a young child.

After he had passed, his daughter Molly had moved in. Newly widowed, she had appeared to share his passion, and had made it her mission to maintain the garden, adding to its splendour over time.

Anna could remember her mother painting in the garden for hours, gifting several of her finished pieces to Molly as a thank you for giving them such an amazing space to share. And Molly being thrilled with each new addition to her collection.

'Anna, what's wrong?'

'The paintings—'

'What about them?'

'They-they're my mum's. I'd recognise her work anywhere.' Grabbing Ben's arm, she took a step closer towards her mother's work and the life she had lost. Ben had no option but to follow.

Anna worked her way slowly around the room, with Ben still attached and following on behind. Her eyes absorbed each signature, her fingers travelling tenderly across the flowing letters. Each painting by the same artist. And all simply signed, *Helena!*

'I-I don't understand. Why are they here? Why would her paintings be here? They're of Edinburgh, our flat, our possessions, the garden, places we walked, places we visited. Why, why would they be here?'

'I-I've no idea.'

Their silence deafening, they stood together. With Anna inspecting every inch of the cluttered walls, Ben appeared uncomfortable and unsure of what he should say or do. All the while, the paintings engulfed Anna, as though her mum were standing by her side.

As the initial shock at discovering her mother's paintings began to ease, Anna lifted her camera, the familiar clicking breaking the silence as she began photographing each painting individually.

Once Anna had worked her way around the room, she began photographing each collection as they adorned the walls, then she turned her attention to the ornaments that were strewn across the various pieces of furniture.

She was only now beginning to take in the layout of the room. The theme was cosy. Dark wooden furniture lifted only slightly by the muted green-and-red checks from the matching curtains, sofa, and armchairs arranged around an open fireplace.

There was nothing unusual in the ornaments. A selection of animal statues – horses, deer, and dogs being the most common.

A few dishes and trinkets and the cast of a rather sizeable fish that she presumed the owner must have caught at some point. But there were no other clues to a past.

Lowering her camera, Anna took a final look around the room before Ben led her back through the bedroom-cum-lounge to the reception area.

'I've no idea what else you might recognise around the place, but if it gets too much or you want to leave, just say.'

Nodding, Anna followed Ben's lead, the reassuring clicking of her camera documenting every square inch as they entered what looked to have been a rather grand sitting room. Situated to the right of the main entrance, it was laid out with various seating areas. Some larger sofas sat around a low, square glass table, ideal for larger groups and families, while small seating areas were scattered around the room for couples or guests who, she presumed, wanted a quieter time.

The furniture and colours were reminiscent of the snug but on a more opulent scale. An open fireplace with an oversized ornate mirror hanging above, unframed and bulky, dominated the far wall. Anna could imagine flames roaring, and guests chatting and laughing, cosy and relaxed while the island winds wrapped around the old bones of the protective building.

The wall to her right had two matching sideboards that were long, dominant, and striking. And probably worth something, too, she thought to herself, so why would they just be left abandoned? The more Anna looked around the room, the more questions she conjured up.

Drawn to the windows facing out from the front of the house, Anna stopped to take in the views spilling down the hillside, across the sparse treetops that led to Lochside and out over the open sea. The North Atlantic shimmered in the distance, the whites of the waves alluding to winter, and a lone power boat skimmed the water as it raced towards the shore.

She stood transfixed by the grandness of the scenery; softer yet just as wild and majestic as her tiny, but precious, part of the island.

Aware of the silence, her thoughts returned to the oddly laid out room. There was a familiarity about it. And imagining the room bustling, she wondered if the various generations had taken the mesmerising views for granted. The thought led her to wonder who had stayed in such a place, and had her mother ever ventured through the doors and gazed out at the same tantalising view?

After all, her mother must have left the photograph of The Old Lodge with her letter for a reason. And it couldn't just be a coincidence that so many of her paintings hung on the walls of the snug.

Working her way slowly around the sitting room, Anna intentionally left the sideboards until last. It was cluttered with photographs, and she was nervous as to who she might see, after her finds in the snug.

Two sofas faced each other on a large central rug, one with its back towards the window. A coffee table bridged the gap. Anna wondered why someone would want to sit with their back towards the views. Her glance fleeted again between the windows and the oddly placed sofa, before settling on the cushions squashed at one end as though someone had just left.

'Was this you?' she said, turning to Ben, who, she noticed, was busy scanning the piece of paper that never left his hand.

'No. But it didn't half unnerve me when I was in here the other day. I felt like someone had run out the back door as I'd come in the front,' he joked.

Continuing around the room, Anna noticed that landscapes covered the walls. All with a look of Skye, and none by her mother. Circling back to the sideboards, Anna braced herself as she searched through the mishmash of frames, all varying in size and containing photographs of people taken inside the lodge and occasionally outside when the weather would allow.

Friends or guests of the owners, she presumed. Given there were no recurring faces, Anna decided she wasn't looking at the owners or their family members.

But everyone was well-dressed, and all the photographs seemed to be years, if not decades, old. Recognising the car from the newspaper articles she had seen in the archive centre, Anna wondered if the room had at one time been used as a function room or a room to entertain, rather than a sitting room.

Ben, still gripping the piece of paper, seemed more interested in the landscapes covering the walls than anything else in the room.

'What *are* you doing?' Anna asked.

'I-I'll tell you once you've finished looking around.'

Again, Anna shrugged. She was overwhelmingly aware of the calming effect the house was having on her. There was a familiarity she couldn't explain, yet she knew she had never been inside before. There was something about the atmosphere that she liked, and the faint aroma that had teased her nostrils since she'd first arrived still reminded her of her mother's wooden box.

Leaving the grandeur of the formal sitting room, Anna followed as Ben led them across the hallway and into the restaurant area. Situated at the left of the main entrance, it enjoyed the same views to the front as the sitting room, and as Anna walked between scattered tables laid with white tablecloths, she could only imagine the room bustling. Waiters and waitresses zigzagging between tables and the room alive with chatter.

An archway in the rear wall led through to a bar and seating area. The bar was in the same dark wood as the reception and just as grand.

'It's like everyone's just disappeared. I-I don't understand.'

'I know, I can't explain it either.' Ben replied.

'And the bar is still stocked. It doesn't make any sense. Why would they just leave everything?'

'Did you see this? I found it the other day.'

'What is it?'

'It's the reservations folder, for dinner.'

Anna's hands scrolled through the pages. A year ago. 'There were people booked in right up until a year ago. What on earth happened?'

'I don't know. But come on, this way.'

Ben led Anna back into the restaurant and through a door at the far end that led into the kitchen at the rear of the house.

'Wow.' Anna couldn't help but smile. The original kitchen was dated but in great condition. The facing wall was dominated by a black Aga. Standing proudly, it was bookended by floor and wall cupboards and a worktop that encircled the room until it met her at either side of the doorway. An old wooden table sat comfortably in front of the Aga. But the centre of the kitchen was kitted out in modern stainless steel, separated into multiple preparation areas before leading to modern ovens, grills, and stoves at the far end.

The original units in the kitchen looked to be handmade, and venturing further, Anna sat at the centre of the old rectangular table, just the type you would expect to find in such a kitchen. Allowing her hands to caress the knots in the wood, she noticed the table was worn smooth, emphasising the passage of time, the age of the house, and all who had filled it.

Ben took the seat beside her. 'It's some place, isn't it?'

'It sure is. I can't explain it, but it—'

'Has a comforting feel, feels like home?'

'Yeah, it really does.'

'I know I've never been here before. My mum's never been back to Skye since the day she left for Aberdeen, so I don't understand why the house makes me feel the way it does.'

'And how is that? How does it make you feel?'

He seemed momentarily lost for an answer. 'I-I don't know! But it's weird, given all that links me to here are old photographs. Photographs that neither of my parents are in. The photograph of you, the fact that my dad hated the place, and that my mum has a key.'

'All I have is an old photograph too. And a photograph of an old couple, who I think might be my grandparents. But then again, they might not be. I mean, the photo might not have been taken here. In fact,'—the thought suddenly dawned on her —'it might not even have been taken on Skye.'

'Come on, you need to see the rest of the house.'

'Wait…why does your mum have a key?'

'I've no idea. She won't tell me!'

Disappointed at Ben's lack of information, Anna followed as he led her back towards the entrance hall.

A large dresser nestled between the two front-facing windows of the restaurant area caught her eye. She stopped to admire the assortment of dishes, plates, cups, saucers, and jugs that had been placed neatly and with purpose. 'Something's off.'

'Huh.'

'Something's off,' she repeated.

'What do you mean?'

'Everything's in its place. No matter what room you go into, everything's as neat as a pin. There's no dust, no cobwebs. The furniture's still polished to within an inch of its life. It's as though the people who live here have simply vanished into thin air. It-it's creepy,' she said, rubbing her hands up her arms to stave off the shivering chill.

'I know what you mean, but I assure you the old guy said no one had lived here for some time. Those were his exact words. *Some time.* He was happy enough for me to look around.'

'But don't you see? It's still immaculate. The restaurant had bookings until a year ago, but someone has hoovered, dusted, and polished in here recently.'

'Yeah, well, you'll change your mind when you go up the stairs.' He scoffed sarcastically.

'Really, show me.'

The sweeping staircase that had stopped Anna in her tracks when they had first entered the lodge now transported them to the first floor. The hallway was carpeted rather than the polished floorboards and ornamental rugs that had been the theme on the ground floor. And the floral wallpaper in greens and golds was even more vibrant when up close, giving a claustrophobic feel.

Anna's camera catalogued the bedrooms as they worked their way along the hall. Each one as tidy as the next – immaculate but dated – with pristinely made beds, en suites, and trays with a kettle, cups, saucers, and a selection of tea and coffee sachets.

All had an assortment of trinkets and paintings, giving each room a personal feel. And all would feel homely, Anna decided, if she were to ignore the eeriness now creeping in after viewing one immaculate yet abandoned bedroom after another.

'Okay, brace yourself for this one.' Ben opened the final door.

It was located at the farthest end of the claustrophobic hallway.

Taking her first tentative step inside, Anna gasped, her hands instinctively cupping her face. 'Wh-what's happened?'

'I don't know.'

'It's like something out of a horror movie.'

'Yup,' Ben replied, making his way further into the room. 'Watch your step. There's broken glass in among all this.'

But Anna was frozen to the spot. And as she surveyed the chaos splayed across the floor in front of her, it was obvious the room had been trashed.

Paintings hung squint. Ornaments, picture frames, and jewellery strewn across the floor as though someone had swept their arm across the chests of drawers and dressing table.

Anna squatted to her knees for a closer look. 'The room has obviously belonged to a female, but the contents are dated, meaning that it's either been unlived in for many years or belonged to a much older woman.'

'Yeah, clothing would have helped solve that puzzle,' Ben agreed. 'Although, there's no dust. Surely if it had been abandoned for years, there would be dust or cobwebs amongst the mess. I mean, there's no way someone is coming in and dusting this chaos.'

'That's true. So, I guess we know an older lady lived in here. And I mean lived. I know there's the obvious owner's quarters downstairs, but there's far too much in here, and it's all too personal to have been open to guests. This had to have been someone's main bedroom.'

'Yeah, you're right. And it's at the end of the hall, so no guests would pass the door. Meaning whoever stayed in here, had privacy.'

Anna's feelings for The Old Lodge had veered between peace and tranquillity, to the eeriness she'd felt as they'd ventured further into the building's secrets, and now to an unsettling and overwhelming sadness that overcame her as she took in the state of the room.

Trying not to disturb anything, she lifted her camera to her eye and began cataloguing the scene, ensuring she covered every inch of the room.

She soon found that viewing the chaos through her lens was helping to distance herself from the emotions the room seemed determined to conjure up. And now, more than ever, she felt they were intruding.

Deciding she would finish clicking the items strewn across the floor then leave, Anna found a safe place to stop and dropped to her knees. The familiar clicking continued to calm her as she documented old photographs fanned out across the floor. Her lens then travelled across bottles of perfume, hairbrushes, and books lying open.

With just a small patch of the floor left to catalogue, Anna allowed her lens to hover over old jewellery, pearls, gold chains, earrings, bracelets, and brooches. Anna's camera continued to click on autopilot, note-taking keeping her occupied just enough to allow her to investigate The Old Lodge without her emotions getting in the way.

She was just getting to her feet when, nestled between a broken picture frame and the chipped lid she presumed was from a small jewellery box, a gold locket caught her eye. Picking it up, she squeezed her nail between the engraved gold edging, forcing the two stiff halves apart.

But no sooner was the locket open than she dropped it to the floor. Her heart skipped. She gasped.

'What's wrong?'

Ben's attention never left his piece of paper.

'It-it's the old couple from my photograph!'

'What.' Ben squatted beside her. 'Are you sure?'

'Yes,' she insisted, retrieving the locket from the chaos, and tilting it so he could take a closer look. 'It's definitely them.'

And as Ben squinted, Anna noticed his reaction mirrored hers. 'What is it?'

'That's the old guy from the cottage up the hill.'

'What? Are-are you sure?'

'Yes, that's definitely him.'

Anna scrambled to her feet. 'I need to speak to him.' And with that, she was running down the stairs towards the main door.

'We'll take my car. Hold on, though, I need to lock up,' Ben called, following behind.

. . .

ANNA FELL INTO THE PASSENGER SEAT OF BEN'S CAR, STILL grasping the locket.

The journey from the lodge to the cottage seemed to take forever. The winding miles of uneven track would have been more suited to her jeep.

Ben had barely stopped when Anna jumped out and knocked on the front door. Ben was just catching up with her when a woman, who Anna guessed to be in her mid-eighties, answered.

The sight of Ben seemed to momentarily unnerve the elderly lady. But she appeared to quickly gather herself as her frame stiffened and expression hardened.

Ben spoke first. 'Sorry to bother you. I'm looking for the gentleman who lives here. I've spoken to him a couple of times over the last few days.'

'He's not here,' she quipped. 'He's gone off for a few days, so he feckin has. Now bugger off.'

Anna, who had been staring at the open locket, broke her silence. 'Is there any way we can contact him? It's important.'

The old woman turned her attention to Anna, her stern composure becoming fractured as she eyed her up and down. 'I have to go,' she replied abruptly, seeming flustered as she turned to close the door.

But Anna, whose thoughts had still been with the lady in the locket, stepped forward. 'Are you his wife?'

'Good heavens, no. I'm his housekeeper.' The woman scowled.

'I have a picture of the gentleman who lives here. It was in my mum's belongings and I'm just trying to work out the link.'

'I can't help you.'

And with that, the door slammed shut. Hearing the lock turning on the other side, Anna knew she had more than struck a nerve with the housekeeper. People rarely locked their doors on the island; they didn't have to, especially in such a remote location as the cottage.

'That woman knew who you were,' Ben raged. 'She recognised you. It was obvious.'

'The man who lives here – did you give him your name or tell him why you were here?'

Ben shook his head. 'He never asked.'

'Don't you think that's odd?'

'Well, not at the time. But now it's bloody strange.'

Anna was now more desperate for answers than ever before. 'What time is it?'

Ben checked his phone. 'Twelve fifteen.'

'Really? Already! We've been here for over two hours, and I haven't seen the whole house yet! And don't forget we've got the archives centre later,' she reminded Ben as they made their way back to his car.

'We'll go back to the lodge for a bit. Let you finish up.'

After a quick three-point turn, he set off towards the lodge.

ANNA WAS JUST FINISHING UP WHEN HUNGER SET IN. BEN WAS obviously feeling the same.

'I don't know about you but my stomach's playing a tune. Why don't we go get some lunch before we head to the archives?' Ben suggested, locking up for a second time.

'Yeah, sure. Let's eat at my place, though, as I need to pick up some things before we speak to Crissie.'

Ben shrugged a nod in agreement.

'Just follow me,' Anna instructed, and they headed back to their vehicles.

Leaving The Old Lodge behind, she turned her attention to the dirt track in front of her. She could see the earth she'd churned up when she'd made her dashes for freedom on the previous two days.

The dust was rising again, swirling around in the cold island wind as she began a less hurried approach down the track.

Watching the dust settle, emphasised by the winter sun against the backdrop of the hillside and the North Atlantic in the distance, Anna was beginning to relax. Sheep were grazing nonchalantly while gulls soared above. It didn't matter where she found herself on the island, the stunning scenery made her feel alive, at home, and ready to embark on whatever the universe decided to throw at her.

And with that, the universe decided to throw a man on a quad bike. A collie, who seemed quite used to this mode of transport, kept the rider company. The quad bike stopped and blocked her way. The rider, cutting the engine, clambered off.

Tall, covered in muck, and in desperate need of a shower, the man approached. A fleeting glance in her rear-view mirror let her know that Ben was following not too far behind.

Locking eyes with the stranger as he neared her side of the jeep, Anna couldn't help but notice his intense chocolate-brown stare. Moody, yet enticing. She struggled to take her eyes off his. Dust from riding the quad bike had settled into the crevices of his features, while short, dark-brown facial stubble met wisps of similarly coloured hair that had escaped the woollen hat so many of the locals wore to stave off the island's chill.

'Can I help you?' she managed, opening her window just enough to hear what he had to say, at the same time deciding he was much younger than she'd first thought. Early-thirties, maybe.

'I'm not sure. Are you with that guy up there?' he said, nodding towards Ben's car.

'I suppose, I mean, well, yes.'

'Mumm, well in that case, I'll tell you what I told him last year. Stay away, stay off the land, and whatever it is you're hoping to gain by sniffing around the lodge, you're not gonna get it. Leave the old man alone. He's been through enough.'

CHAPTER SIX

'Wow, what a spot. It really doesn't matter where you go on this island, does it? I'd have quite liked to have grown up here.'

'I love it,' she gushed. 'I mean, just look.' She pointed towards the dark clouds shrouding the Trotternish Ridge. Majestic in its ruggedness, with faded autumnal colours adding to the mood. 'The island's stunning in all weathers. It doesn't matter where you look. Anyway, let's eat. I'm starving.'

After the morning's discoveries, Anna was relieved to be home. But as she turned her key in the lock, she began to panic about what exactly she could rustle up for lunch. Having decided she was going to The Water's Edge for dinner last night, she had absentmindedly thrown a few essentials into her supermarket trolley, giving more thought to the ice cream and confectionery aisles.

She surveyed the contents of her fridge. 'Okay, so, I'm not all that into cooking. But I can offer you a cheese and ham sandwich or a tin of soup. Oh, or both.' She chuckled, embarrassed at her lack of hostess skills.

'So this is why you always eat at The Water's Edge,' Ben teased, having a quick look around. 'Tell you what, you've plenty eggs, I'll make us cheese and ham omelettes, and you can gather up what you need for this afternoon and check the photos you've taken for any clues.'

'You can't make lunch,' she protested. 'You're a guest.'

'Yes, I can. Anyway, it's the least I can do since you're letting me tag along this afternoon.'

'Okay, thank you,' she replied, eyeing the bowl of eggs – the only staple in her kitchen never to run out, thanks to Mrs Stewart, an elderly neighbour who made it her life's mission to keep Anna stocked with freshly laid eggs.

Connecting her camera to her laptop, Anna began uploading the morning's photographs. Although, she wasn't sure she was ready to look at them. After finding the locket and her mum's paintings, she was worried there could be other clues in the images she had overlooked. And possibly the afternoon was going to be stressful enough, having just discovered a more personal connection to the lodge.

'Frying pan?'

'Cupboard beside the cooker.'

Waiting for her laptop to do its thing, she added a brand-new notepad to her rucksack in preparation for their visit to the archive centre. All the time, a rhythmic chopping came from the kitchen, alerting her to the fact that Ben could cook.

CHAPTER SEVEN

Approaching the archive centre, Anna could feel her stomach flutter. If her theory about the man in the photograph being her grandfather was correct, then he was still alive and living in the cottage at the top of the hill. The reality of which was only just dawning on her.

'I'm not sure I'm going to like what Crissie's about to tell us.' Anna wrapped her scarf around her neck in preparation for the biting winter air. 'If the old man in the cottage is my—'

'It'll be okay,' Ben interrupted. 'We know there is far more to The Old Lodge than we'd first thought, so we just need to be prepared for whatever we find out. And, anyway, I'll be with you.'

Fortunately, Crissie's welcoming smile went some way to putting Anna at ease. 'Hi, Crissie.'

'Hello again.'

'This is Ben. He's…' She was unsure how to end her introduction. Was he a friend? She'd known him all of twenty-four hours. Fortunately, Ben broke her silence.

'Hi, nice to meet you,' he interjected, reaching past Anna to shake Crissie's hand.

'You too, Ben. Follow me.'

Crissie led them towards the search room Anna had been sitting in the previous day. An assortment of paperwork had been arranged in various piles either side of a microfiche.

Crissie signalled for Anna to take a seat while, at the same time, pulling an extra chair across for Ben. 'I've set things out in chronological order, and if you don't mind, we'll stick to that.'

Crissie began by sifting through the pile of papers nearest to her. 'Maren Bay House was built in 1843 by Daniel MacLeod.' She splayed out the relevant paperwork from the time and a photograph of a short, stocky man. He was neither looking happy with his new build nor smiling to the camera. 'This was his wife, Esther. She was from Glasgow and moved to the island when they married. They had seven children but, as was the norm in these days, not all survived.' Crissie produced more photographs, this time of their two surviving daughters and three surviving sons.

Anna and Ben had subconsciously created a system. Anna had delved into her rucksack to retrieve her notepad and was taking notes as Crissie spoke, while Ben was using his mobile to take photos of the newspaper clippings and photographs in the same order that Crissie produced them.

'His eldest son, again called Daniel, took over the house when his parents died. It has since gone down through the generations, always going to the oldest son,' she continued, talking them through the years, producing photographs and articles covering an array of historical events as she went.

Crissie then stopped speaking rather abruptly.

'And what about the current owners?' Anna prompted. 'What has happened to them? We know the lodge has been closed, abandoned almost. Anything you can tell us about them would be helpful.'

Anna recognised the same expression on Crissie's face that

she had noticed the previous day. 'Crissie, what are you not telling me?'

'I think,' Crissie said, her eyes fleeting between Anna and Ben, 'what you're looking for now is more local gossip than historical facts held in the archive. So, I'm afraid I can't help you any further.'

'But you're the only one who can help us.'

'I'm sorry, Anna, but this is my work. I can't just go into hearsay and rumours.'

There was obviously much Crissie still had to say. But Anna understood her predicament. 'It's okay, the last thing we want to do is get you into trouble.'

Rising from her chair, Anna picked up her rucksack and signalled for Ben to follow. 'We really do appreciate everything you've told us.' Anna smiled. 'Thank you so much for your time, Crissie.'

They were just reaching the door when Crissie called after them. 'We close at four thirty. Meet me at Miranda's coffee shop at about four forty-five and we can chat more then.'

ANNA AND BEN SPENT THE NEXT HOUR SITTING AT THE HARBOUR front. Both were cold and restless. The time until they met Crissie again seemed to be taking an eternity to pass. They managed a little light chit-chat as they watched the tide come in, with gulls circling and sailing boats returning from a day on the choppy water, but Anna's heart wasn't in it, and she could sense it was the same for Ben. They were distracted, unsettled, and not much good at cheering each other up.

In their moments of silence, she couldn't help but wonder about Ben. He could be kind. Compassionate almost. But at other times, he was distant, cagey and reluctant to go into his past.

'Where did you learn to cook?'

'What?'

'Where did you learn to cook? I mean you know how to chop; you've obviously been trained.'

'Oh-eh, you know, high school.'

And with that, distant, cagey Ben had returned.

EVENTUALLY, IT WAS TIME TO MAKE THEIR WAY TO MIRANDA'S, and as they entered the café, Anna spotted Crissie sitting in the corner with a woman similar in age.

Waving them over, Crissie stood and began putting her coat back on.

'You're leaving?' Anna questioned.

'Yes, but this is Mairead. She's a good friend of mine and she can help you with what you need to know—'

'Hello, love.'

'Don't worry, you'll be fine,' Crissie said, reaching to open the door. 'And you know where I am if you ever need me.'

It had all become rather serious, as though two loving aunts were making sure their niece was coping after receiving horrendous news. This panicked Anna, given Mairead had still to divulge whatever it was Crissie had been protecting her from.

Miranda appeared to take their order just as Anna and Ben were taking their seats, which lightened the mood a little. 'Hey, Anna. Hot chocolate?'

'Hi, Miranda. Yes, please.'

'Wow, so you're a regular here?' Ben joked.

'Oh, this one's a fan of take-out.' Miranda chuckled.

'I can believe that. I've seen inside her fridge. I'll have the same, thanks.'

Turning to Mairead, Anna guessed she was similar in age to her mother. Goosebumps tingling her arms, Anna braced herself for what she was about to hear. 'Thank you, we really appreciate you speaking to us,' she managed.

'We do,' Ben said. 'Very much.'

'I haven't spoken about this in a long time,' Mairead began. 'But given I know who you are, and who your family are, I'll tell you a little of what I know. But *only* what I know *to be fact.*' She paused. 'I won't be giving you gossip.'

Ben interrupted. 'I'm looking for information too. Anything you might know about my grandparents. My mum is Maggie Sutherland. She moved to—'

'Aberdeen?'

'Yes, how did you know?'

Leaning back in her chair, Mairead ran her fingers through her windblown hair. If she wasn't looking so serious, Anna imagined she would have a pleasant smile, and, she guessed, be quite mischievous. There was a twinkle lurking behind her dead-pan expression.

'How on earth did you two discover each other?'

Anna and Ben locked eyes, confused, concerned, excited.

'We met yesterday at the lodge, or rather, Maren Bay House,' Ben explained.

Observing the wobble in Ben's demeanour, Anna was surprised it unsettled her more than Mairead's comment.

'Well, I suppose I need to start when your parents were young.'

Anna and Ben leaned in.

'Iain MacLeod, your grandfather'—Mairead nodded towards Anna—'came from a long line of sheep crofters. As a family croft, they had done quite well for themselves through the generations. But let's go back to when your great-grandfather ran the croft. Maren Bay House or The Old Lodge, as we call it, was their family home at that time.' Mairead nodded to Anna, ensuring she was keeping up. 'One summer when your grandfather was in his early twenties, your great-grandfather sent him off to a croft on the mainland. A crofter friend of your great-grandfather's had taken unwell and needed the extra help. When your grandfather returned a year or so later, your grandmother, Susanna, was with him.'

'S-Susanna?' Anna questioned, a shiver running down her spine.

Mairead nodded. 'Yes, Susanna. You didn't know?'

Anna shook her head.

'Oh, oh dear. Well, you were named after your grandmother. I know that for a fact.'

'I'd no idea,' Anna replied, finally understanding why her mother had insisted she only ever be known as Anna.

This latest discovery was making Anna realise just how unprepared she was for whatever she was about to uncover. And while panic set in, so did the overwhelming realisation that there was no turning back.

Mairead's uncomfortable attempt to move the conversation on was obvious. 'Well, she had lived in a neighbouring village and had dated your grandfather for much of the time he was on the mainland. It was Susanna who eventually transformed The Old Lodge into what it is now and renamed it Maren Bay House.' Mairead smiled. 'She oversaw the extension and renovation of the place. She could see the building's potential and brought it up to its current state. It seemed she found island life too quiet and wanted something to do that was hers, so once the extension was complete, she opened the house up as a country hotel.'

Mairead stopped to sip her coffee. 'And things seemed fine. Your grandparents seemed to have a happy marriage, obviously very much in love. And, eventually, after many years of trying, they had your mum.'

Anna, who had been hanging on Mairead's every word, interjected. 'I feel a *but* coming.'

'Ah, well, it does all unravel a bit from there. Look, love.'
She smiled. 'I said earlier I'd not be giving you gossip, and I
won't be. But knowing your mum as I did, she'd want me to tell
you the bits I know to be fact.'

'You knew my mum?'

Mairead placed a hand on Anna's arm. 'All in good time,
love. We'll get to that part soon, I promise.' She took the final
sip of her coffee and continued. 'One year, we had an unusually
bad winter. Your grandfather lost some of his flock – quite a bit,
actually – and at the same time, the weather had caused exten-
sive damage to the croft cottage and outbuildings. The cottage
being as exposed as it is up there, you know—'

'You mean the cottage at the top of the hill, above the
lodge?' Ben interrupted.

'Yes, that's the one. It caused the money to dry up. After a
few years of struggling, they were forced to sell off some of the
land. It caused a rift between your grandparents for a good long
while as, at the time, the lodge was doing well. I think your
grandfather expected Susanna to sell it, to help keep the croft,
but she never did. Your grandmother had money, and a lot of it.
She was from a wealthy family on the mainland. Obviously
knew what she was doing when it came to the financial side of
things, and she kept the lodge separate from the croft. Protected
it, I guess. Running a croft eats through the money, you know.
And any unexpected losses can be a disaster for many.'

'So, what happened?' Ben asked.

'Well, all's I know is that after selling off some of the land,
your grandfather kept the cottage up the hill and enough land
to work a reasonably sized croft. But—' She looked at Anna.

'But what?'

'The only buyer at the time was—'

'Who?' Anna prompted.

'The owners of the croft your grandfather had helped on
the mainland all these years before. Your—' Mairead lowered

her eyes, rubbing her hands together as if it would make her disappear.

Aware of Mairead's discomfort, Anna was, for the first time, beginning to wonder if she didn't want to hear what Mairead was about to say. But it was too late. No sooner had she had the thought than Mairead's trapped words came spilling out.

'Your *other* grandfather!'

Anna's hands recoiled to cup her face.

Ben put his arm around her, apparently trying to comfort her as best he could, but Anna was now wiping at silent tears.

'She doesn't know who her father is,' Ben interjected.

'I know. Well, I mean, I presumed as much. After Crissie phoned me last night to ask if I'd be willing to speak to you both, I made a few calls, confidentially of course,' she assured, 'and tried to confirm as much as I possibly could about what I know.'

Anna managed a nod.

'Anna, when your mum and dad had a bit of a fling, it only lasted a few months. You see, your grandfathers had never gotten along. Something had upset their fathers, and your grandfathers only ever knew each other as rivals. It was common knowledge. Everyone knew about the rivalry between the two families who'd once been firm friends, and both families were prepared for trouble when your mum and dad got together.'

Mairead shifted awkwardly in her chair. 'Anna, I knew your mother. She was a couple of years younger than me, but she was friendly with my younger sister. They went through school together. I can remember your mum as clear as day. She spent a lot of time at our house when we were growing up.'

Mairead hung her head. 'I'm so sorry, Anna, but it was me who accompanied your mum to Edinburgh the day she left the island.'

Unsure of how she should reply, Anna listened as tears

soaked her cheeks and an ache in her stomach reminded her of how she had felt in the days and weeks after her mother's death.

'Your grandmother had a friend in Edinburgh, Sheona Macdonald. She'd gone to school with my mother and your grandmother and the three of them had kept in touch. I had been to visit her with my mum a couple of times, so your grandmother asked if I would accompany your mum as she had never been off the island before.' Mairead fell silent again, as though searching for the correct words. 'Your mum was distraught the day she left. We were sitting about halfway back in a horrible old bus. She was cold, had been sick with morning sickness not long before we left, and the long bus journey did nothing to help that, at all. It was a rough journey for your mum.'

Anna couldn't bear the thought of her mother being so upset or going through such a horrific journey. And as she thought back to the gentle, loving, kind, and funny person she had known her mother to be, Anna felt proud of who her mother had become. How she had overcome such unsettling events and had flourished in a city she had learned to love and genuinely called home.

Realising she had slumped in her chair, Anna composed herself. Sitting up straight, she searched her bag for a tissue and wiped her eyes and nose.

'I can't tell you what it means to speak to someone who knew my mum, especially back then. It'— she sniffled—'it helps keep her alive in my mind, having someone to speak to, hearing about her past. Other than Rob and Andy, I've no one.' She sobbed.

She removed her layers as the warmth of the building fought with her padded jacket, and she ran her fingers through her hair as if she were hitting the reset button. 'Where's your sister now, Mairead?'

'Nancy emigrated to New Zealand a long while back. She

and her husband both have good jobs and no kids, so they visit every couple of years. Before your mum became unwell, they would often start their journey home by flying out of Edinburgh, just so Nancy could meet up with your mum. They'd quite a few reunions over the years. Stayed close, you know.'

Anna managed a smile and was grateful that her mother had had such a friendship and a link to her childhood. But at the same time, she was struggling to understand her mother's secrecy surrounding her past and her connection to the island. Never in all their years together had Anna heard about a friend in New Zealand.

'You okay, love?'

'I don't understand. Why all the secrecy?'

'Around your mother's past?'

'Yes.'

'I don't know, love. I really don't.'

'But you know who her grandparents are?' Ben interrupted.

She nodded. 'Yes, yes, I do.' Fidgeting with her teaspoon, she said, 'Both of your grandfathers are still alive. They live quite close to each other, actually.'

'The man in the cottage at the top of the hill, above the lodge. Is he one of them?' Ben asked.

She nodded. 'Yes. That's Helena's father. He, eh—'

Aware Mairead was feeling awkward, Anna gave her a pleading smile.

'I phoned him last night, too. Told him I might be speaking to you today. I needed to know what I could tell you. This is no longer history from an archive centre, love. This is people's lives. It's now other people's story to tell.'

'I know, I'm sorry, we don't mean to put you in a position. It's just we knew nothing before. And knowing absolutely nothing about my family tree, where I've come from, on either of my parents' sides, has felt unbearably lonely since my mum passed away. I've no little family anecdotes,' Anna continued. 'No historical stories or tales. There's no loft full of our family's past, or photograph albums. I've known nothing my entire life.'

'Well,' Mairead said, an awkwardness coming over her, 'your grandfather told me I should tell you who he is and everything I know. But I told him I wasn't comfortable telling you any more about your family than I already have. It's not my place. It's his. I've only told you what I know Helena would want you to hear. My sister and I owed her that much. Anything else is up to your grandfathers.'

Mairead began putting on her coat.

'But, what about my other grandfather?' Anna asked, a little louder than she'd intended.

'I haven't spoken to him. He's not someone I could just phone up about this. I don't know him all that well. He's the quiet kind, keeps himself to himself. But, if you manage to speak to your other grandfather, the one at the top of the hill, he'll be able to tell you everything you want to know.'

'But that will be a biased view, will it not?' Ben interjected.

'I think enough time, and enough grief, has passed. After speaking to him last night, I'm sure he'll be fine. And, I don't mean any disrespect, Anna, but your mum could be stubborn and feisty, especially with your grandfather. She didn't make things easy for herself and she made it difficult for your grandfather any time he tried to make peace. I'm telling you this because you have a chance at finding your family. I just don't want you having your guard up unnecessarily when it comes to your grandfather, Iain MacLeod. Just give him a chance, please.'

'He's gone away for a few days.'

'What?'

Mairead's surprise was evident in her tone.

'We spoke to his housekeeper this morning.'

'His housekeeper?'

'Yes, she answered his door to us today.'

It was obvious that Mairead knew there was more to the housekeeper than met the eye. 'Is there something you're not telling us about the housekeeper?' Anna asked.

'Well, yes, but I think it should come from your grandfather. So, please, give him a chance.' She reached for Anna's pen and wrote her mobile number beneath her notes. 'I'll still be here any time you want to chat,' she promised, clasping Anna's hand in hers. 'But first, speak to your grandfather. It's only fair.'

Nodding, Anna gave Mairead a hug. 'Thank you. We'll go back and speak to the housekeeper in the morning.'

'I think that's a good idea.' Mairead smiled.

'But what about my mum's family?' Ben pleaded. 'There has to be something you can tell me before you go? Do I have any connections to the lodge?'

She glanced back and forth between Ben and Anna. 'You two really only met yesterday? And for the first time?'

'Yes,' they both echoed.

'Are we related?'

'No, you're not related. Your mums were best friends growing up. Inseparable, you never saw one without the other. So, I knew your mum, too, Ben, just as well as I knew Helena. You must remember this was a long time ago, before the hordes of day trippers and holidaymakers. The island community was small. We all knew each other…'

'What is it?' Ben urged.

'I guess it's all going to come out when you talk to the'— Mairead made a face—'when you talk to the housekeeper.'

'She knows my mum?'

But Mairead didn't seem to register his question.

'Your dad, is he still around?'

'Yes, well, no. I mean he's still alive, if that's what you mean, but we have nothing to do with him. I haven't seen him in years.'

'Hmmm.' Mairead squinted at Ben. 'We've met you know, many years ago. You were just a young lad, at primary school, the last time I saw you. Nancy and I were over in Inverness, and we paid your mum a visit. I'd never have recognised you now, though.' She appeared thoughtful. 'Okay, well, anyway, go back, and speak to the'—she rolled her eyes—'the housekeeper. You both deserve to know where you're from, especially now. Enough time has surely passed, for goodness' sake. And, if she won't speak to you, your grandfather will, Anna. I'm guessing he just needs time. It will be painful for him to speak about the past.'

'But he was the cause of all the pain, was he not? He was the reason my mum left?'

'Oh, I'd say your mum had a lot to do with it, but that's just my understanding.'

'Okay, but you know who my dad is, don't you?' Anna hurriedly asked as Mairead made her way towards the door.

'Look, when it comes to the topic of fathers, that's not my place. I've said enough, probably too much. But I knew Helena, and I know she wouldn't want you to be alone in this world. She would want you to find your family, find your roots, and they're here. They're here for you both.'

'Before you go.' Ben was out of his chair and following Mairead to the door. 'My mum has a key to Maren Bay House. Do you know why?'

'She has a key.' Mairead laughed. 'Lordy, well done her. She used to clean the lodge. It was before your mother left, Anna, and for a bit afterwards, but Maggie was a devil in her time. She was the mischievous one, never any fear. She used to give your grandfather a hard time too. She was sharp tongued and never forgave him for your mother leaving. And she'd remind him of it often with her comments.'

'So, that's why my photograph's on Ben's mum's mantelpiece? Because she and my mum were friends?'

Nodding, Mairead turned to Ben. 'Your mother didn't have an easy childhood. Anna's grandfather knew that, and folks were often surprised at what he let her get away with. Your grandfather could have a soft heart at times, Anna. Unfortunately, he just didn't always know how, or when, to show it.'

CHAPTER EIGHT

Exhausted, Anna and Ben fell into their chairs at The Water's Edge. Having found a table close to the fire, Anna was leaning back, eyes closed, absorbing the heat, when Rob appeared.

'Susie, Susie, thank goodness.'

Jumping to her feet, she gave Rob a hug.

'You've been so quiet. No calls, no texts. We were starting to worry.'

'Sorry, it's been a strange day. But we've lots to tell you.'

'We?' Rob raised an eyebrow towards Ben.

Laughing at Rob's attempt at the macho father figure, Anna began introducing the two officially. 'Ben, this is Rob.'

'Hello, Rob. Nice to meet you.' Ben jumped to his feet, his hand outstretched.

'Rob, this is Ben.'

'Hmm.' Rob turned his attention back to Anna. 'You've lots to tell us, huh?'

'It turns out our mothers were close friends,' Anna explained.

'Oh.' Rob's attention was now well and truly grasped as he pulled a chair for himself from the neighbouring table, all the while keeping his eyes on Ben. 'Well, come on then, tell me who you are and where you have hailed from at this impressively opportunistic moment.'

'Rob,' Anna scolded.

'I'm sorry, Susie,' he said mockingly. 'Is that not what a dad would say?'

Anna stifled a chuckle. She knew Rob was relishing the moment while Ben was squirming uncomfortably in his chair, wondering what the hell was going on.

'I thought you didn't know your dad,' Ben interrupted.

'I don't.' She laughed. 'This is Rob. He, his husband Andy, and my mum were best friends. Rob and Andy are like family to me.' Reaching over, she hugged Rob's arm. 'They are my family.'

'Yes,' Rob said, squinting at Ben. His demeanour changed, shoulders stiffening. 'I'm the hell you'll have to deal with if you hurt our Susie.'

While Ben's panicked eyes darted back and forth between the two of them, Anna struggled to keep her face serious. Eventually she fell into fits of laughter, jokingly telling Rob to be nice. And Rob, failing to keep up the pretence, was soon echoing Anna in a fit of giggles.

Rob rose from his chair. 'Well, I think I've caused enough trouble for one night.' And handing them each a menu, he said, 'I'll come back in a few minutes to take your order.'

'Okay, so who the hell was that?' Ben demanded as soon as Rob was out of earshot. 'And what's with the *Susie*?'

A little taken aback at his tone, Anna filled him in. Rob and Andy first met my mum when they came to view The Water's Edge. They got chatting to her in a café. I was just a toddler. And the rest is history.' She shrugged. 'They became like brothers to her. They were her family. She was secretive though'—Anna paused—'never discussing her past, not even with them.'

. . .

SHE WAS IN THE MIDDLE OF EXPLAINING HER UNCONVENTIONAL yet immensely valuable little family when Rob re-appeared with a glass of Merlot and a pint of Tennent's.

'On the house,' he said, giving Ben a cheeky wink. 'Right, are you two ready to order?'

A quick glance at the specials, and Anna and Ben both opted for the lamb.

'Good choice. It won't be long. Oh, Anna, can you hang around when you're done? Andy would like a chat when the rush is over.'

'Yeah, sure.'

Appearing grateful of that first sip, Ben watched Rob as he went off to clear a couple of tables. 'He's larger than life, is he not?'

'He's just winding you up. If you stick around long enough to get to know him and Andy, you'll realise they're both gentle giants. Protective of me, though.'

They devoured their lamb and followed it with an Eton mess and chocolate tart. The sight of Ben's pudding had led Anna to regret her choice, and he'd been kind enough to share. Over their meal, they dissected the information Crissie and Mairead had given them earlier, and they discussed the photographs Ben had taken of Crissie's records at the archive centre.

They both agreed they would only get more information from Mairead if Anna's grandfather refused to talk, and both were now suspicious of the so-called housekeeper.

But Anna was also nervously skirting around the fact that The Old Lodge had obviously been a significant part of both their mothers' lives on the island. And then there was Mairead's comment about Anna's grandfather having a soft spot for Maggie. Was there more to that story than Mairead had let on?

'Same again?' Ben asked, getting to his feet.

'Eh, no. Can I have a coffee please?' She smiled, suddenly aware of how busy the restaurant had become.

As Ben took his place in the queue at the bar, Anna noticed him looking around, craning his neck to see into the nooks and crannies of the restaurant. It seemed he was looking for someone. And given she was sure he knew no one on the island other than those he had met through Anna, his behaviour was enough to unsettle her. And the more she watched him as he stepped forward in the queue, the more convinced she was that he was seeking someone in particular.

Why did she swing back and forth on her opinion of him? she wondered. How could she be so at ease in his company one minute and yet so ready to presume he was up to no good the next? But deep down she knew there was something about him that unsettled her; she just couldn't put her finger on what.

A man, similar in age to Ben, making a discreet entrance was enough to pull her from the thoughts. Ben had noticed him too, and Anna watched as the two men seemed to silently acknowledge each other before the stranger was shown to a table.

'Are you okay?' she asked, as Ben returned to his seat. 'I mean you seemed to know that guy who came in.'

'What? No. No, I don't know anyone here, just you,' he quipped. 'Anyway, I think I'll head after this. It's been a long day. You okay to get yourself home?'

'Eh, yeah, sure. I need to finish mounting and framing some photographs for the galleries anyway.'

'Okay,' he replied, downing the last of his pint. 'I'll see you in the morning.'

And as Ben made his hasty retreat, Anna's eyes were on the stranger, who, she decided, didn't look too dissimilar to Ben!

CHAPTER NINE

Anna had paid particular attention to her hair and make-up, was wearing her favourite blue jeans, and had chosen a top that was modern and flattering instead of the usual fleeces and woolly jumpers that were her norm at this time of year on the island. A long, grey chunky cardigan and dress boots finished her ensemble. And taking one last look in the mirror, she surprised herself at the amount of effort she had put in. But if they were to win over the housekeeper, Anna knew she needed to feel as confident, and be as assertive, as possible.

And with her jeep loaded and ready to make her deliveries later that afternoon to the few galleries and stockists that remained open on the island during the winter, Anna set off for The Old Lodge. The low winter sun shimmering across a crisp blue sky served only to remind Anna of the island's beauty and how effortlessly it had become her home from home. Although this morning, it was to be short-lived. With torrential rain and strong winds forecast to come in around lunchtime, Anna hoped to have spoken with the housekeeper and made her deliveries before the bad weather arrived. Her deliveries to the mainland could wait until another day.

To Anna, the weather didn't matter. Whether the Quiraing was shrouded in sunshine, looming tall in torrential rain, or standing its ground in hundred mile-an-hour winds, it was dramatic, beautiful, and utterly breathtaking. And she had the privilege of soaking in its beauty every single day. Something she never tired of.

The road from Staffin to Portree was just as stunning. Slowing down to allow the resident sheep to pass freely was not an unusual occurrence, this morning being no different. A few stragglers bleated a thank you as they meandered nonchalantly by, and Anna often enjoyed slowing to a stop to watch them on their way.

This morning, it was a delivery lorry that brought her to a halt. Her jeep had the benefit of giving her height; she could see the road ahead clearer than those in lower cars and was aware of a small car and run-down Land Rover following on behind. Sitting tight in her passing bay, she waited patiently. The lorry slowed to a crawl as it squeezed itself between Anna's jeep and the huddle of sheep lying by the other side of the road, oblivious to the chaos they were causing.

Keeping his eyes on the road, the delivery driver gave her an acknowledging wave of thanks, as did the smaller car following on behind. Instinctively, Anna went to give the driver of the run-down Land Rover the same *You're welcome* wave as she had the previous two drivers, when he slowed to a stop.

The expressionless face staring back at Anna startled her until she recognised the moody yet enticing brown eyes of the driver who'd blocked her way with the quad bike the day before.

The melting pools of brown lingered on her for what felt like an eternity, before the man drove off without a word, wave, or hint of acknowledgement.

Anna's high spirits had gone. She was left rattled, flustered, and intimidated by the actions of the stranger who had alluded to a previous conversation with Ben. Making a mental note to quiz Ben about him later, Anna continued into Portree.

Following the road towards the harbour and through town, Anna reached the roundabout that welcomed most drivers as they arrived in Portree. A quick decision was needed. She could head north-west, followed by a quick left, along a road she loved. Or she could simply continue north-west along the main road to Dunvegan.

Turning left would allow her to cross rugged countryside that would undoubtedly be stunning in the current weather conditions, along a single-track road dappled with passing places.

She knew the island well enough to know the bright winter sky would be reflected on the River Snizort, while the remote landscape with its meandering sheep would provide photography opportunities in abundance, especially if the tide was in as she met the sea loch at Struan. The lure to pull over and photograph the island's remote splendour would, she knew, be irresistible.

With that in mind, she reluctantly continued along the main road out of Portree before turning west at Borve. The road to Dunvegan was one she knew well, and as she fell into the flow of the intermittent traffic, the photography opportunities would become less of a distraction.

Her thoughts soon turned to the so-called housekeeper. Anna was more than aware they would need her on-side if they were to stand any chance of getting her to admit her real identity or speak to them at all, for that matter. But she worried that might be easier said than done. And then there was all she might divulge about The Old Lodge, its past, and the man Anna now knew was her grandfather. The very thought unnerved her. After speaking with Mairead, Anna wasn't sure she was ready to hear all that the housekeeper might have to say.

The more Anna thought about her grandfather, the more relieved she was to know he wouldn't be there. Not least because the housekeeper might be more inclined to speak to them if she were alone. Deep down, Anna knew she wasn't ready to meet the man who had caused her mother to leave everything and everyone she had known.

But, as she continued towards Dunvegan, the island's beauty insisted on distracting her with picture-perfect opportunities. The cold, crisp morning was capped by an ocean-blue sky dappled with circling gulls, buzzards, and what might have been a sea eagle, if she'd had the time to stop and look through her lens.

Arriving in Dunvegan, Anna continued south towards the lodge. But not before a quick glance in the direction of Dunvegan Castle, a road she would take often when across this side of the island. She loved nothing more than leaving the tourists behind as she continued past the castle and along the coastal road towards one of her many favourite spots on the island.

She would set up her camera and wait as she looked out over Loch Dunvegan and its sprinkling of tiny, rocky islands. The lolloping seals were often happy to pose as they bathed on the rocks. Resident herons would wander into shot as they fished along the shoreline, while oystercatchers made the most of the rock pools revealed by the receding tide.

But knowing she needed to focus on the topic at hand, Anna continued south towards the lodge. But not before deciding that half an hour spent photographing the sea loch from Abigail's jetty, followed by a chat with her friend, would be an ideal way to relax after she and Ben finished speaking to the housekeeper. A bit of much-needed chill time before making her deliveries to the various galleries.

CHAPTER TEN

Having left her ageing jeep at The Old Lodge, Anna braced herself while Ben's car ricocheted off every bump, dip, and crevice of the rugged track leading up to the cottage.

'She might not open the door, you know,' Ben remarked.

'I know.' Anna's heart sank at the thought, after all the effort she'd put into her appearance, while at the same time she wished she'd insisted they take her jeep.

But, finally, Ben pulled up outside the cottage, and Anna's whitened knuckles released themselves from the door handle.

'You look nice,' Ben said as they made their way towards the door.

'Thank you.' But noticing Ben's choice of clothing was, again, more in keeping with someone who worked in a city office, Anna felt herself becoming annoyed. His smart, straight trousers and dress shoes could not have looked more out of place as they walked towards the cottage at the top of a windy hill. Especially given the splattering of sheep droppings splayed across the track in front of them.

But it was the shirt and tie lurking beneath the woollen dress coat that meant he looked even more out of place on the island than usual. And as she watched him step tentatively between the sheep droppings that islanders took for granted, she began to feel uncomfortable. The niggling feeling she had been unable to shake when they had first met was often lost in his politeness and chivalry, but watching him approach the door, her hackles were raised, once again.

And the more she looked, the more she realised the quality of his clothing didn't quite match his shiny, black car. And although his choice of clothing was that of a professional working in an upmarket office in the city, the quality was poor. Threads hung from the hem of his coat. His shirt collar didn't quite sit as it should, and his shoes – not leather – looked brand-new. The more she thought about it, the more unsettled she became.

Convinced his choice of clothing was more an act than a reflection of his working life, she asked, 'What do you do?'

'What?'

He knocked at the door.

'Your job. What do you do?'

'Oh, I'm, eh…'

Another knock.

'Oh, I think I hear someone.'

The key turning in the lock ended their conversation.

The housekeeper only partially opened the door, and on seeing Anna and Ben, was about to close it without uttering a single word, when Anna interjected. 'Please, please speak to us. I'm begging you. We know you're more than the housekeeper, and I'm desperately needing answers about my mum and her life on the island. Please?'

'He-he isn't here.'

'That's okay. I would really like to speak to you, if you don't mind. We've been to the archive centre. We know you can help us.'

The housekeeper's shoulders rounded as her eyes dropped

to her feet. Anna had the impression that if they could encourage her to speak, she would be a wealth of information.

Noticing Ben was unusually quiet, Anna continued. 'I found a locket in the lodge. It contains the picture of a couple. My mum left a photograph of the same couple with a letter I found after she passed away. But the letter didn't mention who they were. I was hoping you could—'

But teardrops landing on the doorstep stopped Anna mid-sentence. The housekeeper's hunched shoulders lowered as she discreetly dried her eyes. Anna placed a comforting hand on her arm. 'I'm so sorry. We didn't mean to upset you. We really didn't. We just hoped you could help us unravel our past, that's all,' she said, her hand still rubbing gently, assuring the housekeeper.

The housekeeper straightened herself, wrenched her arm from Anna's comforting strokes, and tucked her grey hair sternly behind her ears. 'You're Susanna, aren't you?'

'Yes. Susanna MacLeod.' A thudding rose in her chest. Calming herself, Anna dared to ask the question. 'How do you know my full name?'

'You'd better come in.'

A gentle shove in the base of her spine was needed as Ben encouraged Anna to follow the housekeeper inside. Although the cottage was dwarfed by the surrounding landscape, the rooms felt surprisingly spacious.

Following the housekeeper into the kitchen, Anna caught the faintest whiff of the familiar smell.

'Tea?'

'Yes, please,' Ben replied. 'Just milk, for both of us.'

Taken aback that he would answer for her, Anna glanced fleetingly at Ben before turning her attention back to the house-keeper. 'Just a little for me, please.'

'Sit,' their host instructed sharply, nodding towards the farthest end of a wooden table that filled the room.

Ben gestured for Anna to sit, and following his instructions, she chose the seat nearest to her. She was aware of the empty chairs between them, but her legs had gone limp, refusing to allow her to venture any further. Steadying her breathing, she watched as the elderly lady made the tea.

Anna could tell the housekeeper had been attractive in her time. Soft features and elegantly dressed, she was obviously someone who had looked after herself.

A plate of biscuits appeared on the table, placed strategically between her and Ben. A mixture of shortbread and chocolate chip cookies, it reminded her of Edinburgh and of life with her mum.

Anna watched their host. Arthritis had ravaged her hands, making the simplest of tasks appear troublesome. Which, mixed with her lack of eye contact, meant Anna was becoming concerned. She knew their appearance had upset the housekeeper, but added to her age and frailty, Anna felt they should tread carefully.

Taking in the rest of the room, Anna noticed a large Aga dominated the far wall. Socks hung on the rail to dry, as did gloves and an old woollen hat. The kitchen looked new, although fitted out in a traditional style. A mixture of duck-egg blue and oak gave a warm, homely feel, while the table encircled with ten oak chairs suggested many visitors.

The rear door and kitchen window looked out over the hillside. Anna could see sheep grazing on grass just a few feet from the cottage, while a buzzard circled in the distance. The blue sky that had accompanied her across the island was now looking dull and grey as murky clouds rolled in, leading Anna to wonder if the bad weather was coming in sooner than forecast.

Finally, their host poured the tea and settled herself in a chair opposite Anna, as if needing the protective barrier of the table.

Anna spoke first. 'I'm sorry we upset you. We didn't mean

to. We just wondered if you could answer a few questions, help us find out who we are and how we are connected to the lodge and the couple in the locket. But, firstly, can we ask your name?'

A sigh escaped the elderly lady in response, in an unnervingly similar way to that of Anna's mother.

'Please?'

'My name is Sarah.' She looked at Anna properly for the first time since they had arrived. 'I'm your grandfather's sister. Your great-aunt.'

Anna felt her face redden, and the thudding in her chest returned. 'So, it's true. The man who lives here is my grandfather?'

Nodding, Sarah sipped her tea.

Tears continued to dampen Sarah's cheeks, and Anna absorbed every minute detail of her newly found great-aunt. And as she did so, churning welled in her stomach. A feeling of dread spread through her, rendering her speechless. She couldn't shake the feeling that Sarah's tears were more for the fact she had been discovered than the appearance of her great-niece. Bracing herself, Anna knew there was going to be no happy family reunion. No delight at her sudden appearance, and given her feelings about her grandfather, no extended family to be gained.

And the more Anna looked, the more she saw the similarities. Sarah's cheekbones, not dissimilar to her mother's. The way she clasped her hands, although old and arthritic, her movements like that of her mother.

But with their silence deafening, Anna realised they would get nowhere unless they coaxed out more. And no matter what apprehensions Anna may have had, she was here now. This was her moment to uncover what she could about her mother's past and her links to the lodge. Taking a breath, she said, 'If-if you're my great-aunt, then you were my mum's aunt.' Anna stuttered. 'There must be so much you can tell us.'

Sarah gave a scoff, which confused Anna. Sarah had invited them in, made them tea. And to what purpose, if she wasn't prepared to tell them anything? Starting to feel like an intruder, Anna was beginning to wonder if she and Ben should leave when Sarah interrupted her thoughts.

'Yes, I was…am. I'm your mum's aunt.'

Ageing, watery blue eyes stared back at her own, emphasising to Anna the enormity of the moment. She had found a living relative. Past events were momentarily forgotten as she studied every crevice of Sarah's face.

Finally, a branch to her family tree. Minute and fragile, but it was there, sending echoes of a past, a history, a belonging. Desperate for Sarah to divulge more of her world, yet terrified at what she might say.

Seconds felt like minutes, minutes like hours, the uninterrupted silence deafening, as a cacophony of questions invaded Anna's thoughts.

Ben finally found his voice. 'Is there anything you can tell us?'

Sarah's eyes, fragile with age yet hard in their stare, turned towards Ben. 'Who did you say you were?' she stuttered.

Appearing reluctant to answer, he said, 'I-I'm Ben.'

'Ben who?'

'Just Ben.'

Sarah's eyes bore further into Ben's. 'Just Ben, hmmm? I'm not inclined to trust a man with no last name.'

A mere shrug from Ben surprised Anna. She had expected him to leap into his usual spiel about his mum and how she had moved to Aberdeen. Instead, he remained silent, leaving Sarah appearing more upset by his appearance than Anna's.

Feeling the need to break the awkward silence, Anna interrupted. 'Could we ask you some questions?'

'I promised him I wouldn't tell you, but you said you've been to the archive centre.' Sarah dabbed her eyes again. 'It's far better you hear the whole sodding tale from me than the feckin gossips in town.'

Anna leaned forward, her gaze firmly fixed on Sarah, willing her to continue with every ounce of her being. But the rear door opening stopped Sarah in her tracks.

Caught off guard, Anna was met with the same moody yet enticing stare that had so coolly bored into her earlier that morning. But the man's cool exterior appeared to crack when he noticed Ben sitting at the farthest end of the table.

'It's fine, Hamish. Just go,' Sarah instructed, pouring tea into a Thermos cup and handing it to him along with biscuits from the table. 'I said, go. For feck sake, just go,' she reiterated loudly, her frail hand gesturing towards the door.

But a slight change in the man's expression seemed enough to unsettle Ben, and Anna could only watch as Hamish's unspoken warning appeared to have far more impact than any words.

'Now, Hamish,' Sarah insisted, releasing Ben from the moment.

Taken aback at Sarah's abruptness, Anna watched as Hamish retreated reluctantly towards the door, his attention turning to her as he did so. The icy stare that had moments before held Ben in such disdain had softened. And Anna felt herself flush as his gaze held hers until the winter winds evaporated behind the closing door.

'You must have many questions,' Sarah interrupted, 'and you have to know you're often in my thoughts, especially since your mum—'

Anna sat motionless. Silent. To hear she was often in her great-aunt's thoughts struck like a dagger. Often in her thoughts, but not enough to make any attempt to see her, make sure she was okay, or comfort her after the loss of her mother.

'I thought about going to see the two men who run The Water's Edge. I know Helena was friendly with them, but too much time had passed. She was my niece,' Sarah exclaimed, tears streaming down her cheeks, 'and we were close, at times, until she left for Edinburgh. But she never forgave me for staying quiet and not standing up for her.'

Surprised at her comment, Anna couldn't imagine Sarah having trouble standing up to anyone. Certainly not from what she had seen of her great-aunt so far, anyway.

Sarah continued, her frail hands wiping at her cheeks. 'But-but how could I? My brother's never been the easiest man to get along with. Still isn't,' she added, giving Anna a sideways glance.

Always the first to comfort anyone, Anna knew the words needed to offer solace to her newly discovered relative, yet they choked in her throat. Anna sat in disbelief as Sarah continued to ramble on about her past, and how her own lonely life had meant she'd been unable to help her niece.

Anna thought about the bus trip her mum had endured and how terrified she must have felt leaving the remoteness of the island for a bustling city she had never seen. Pregnant and disowned by a father who'd appeared to put his rivalry before his own family, his own daughter.

And then there was her grandmother, who it seemed had stood back, quietly allowing it all to happen, even orchestrating the trip. Yes, she had paid for the flat in Edinburgh. Yes, she had paid for Anna to go to university. And, yes, she had made sure Anna and her mother were financially secure, but Anna knew deep down that all her mother had ever wanted was a loving family.

As tears escaped Anna's eyes, she watched the elderly woman sitting across from her. Still speaking, still coming out with excuses as to why she left Anna to deal with her mother's death without family around her. Why she had left Anna to struggle on, grieving for a mother she adored and lost all too soon.

Sarah unburdened her guilt on Anna without so much as asking how she was. How she had coped. How she had kept going in what had become a lonely and desolate world. Sarah's ramblings continued, unbearable, utterly selfish and void of sympathy for anyone other than herself.

It was becoming too much. The room became claustrophobic. Ben seemed oblivious. Sarah's deluge continued. Anna's chest beat faster. Her stomach lurching, she felt nauseous. Panic rising, her body hot, she struggled to breathe. Rising from her chair, she ran out through the rear door, gulping in the cold winter air. The dark, murky clouds had given way to drizzle, its damp mist cooling her flushed cheeks.

Momentarily disorientated, Anna ran to the front of the house and down the track away from the excuses of a relative whose only concern appeared to be that of relieving herself of her own guilt. A great-aunt who had chosen to leave her abandoned in a lonely world.

Anna could hear Ben's car churning up the track as he neared. She reached for the handle and was shocked to find the door locked. Expecting him to flick the button that would unlock the car, she waited, only for him to roll down the window.

'I'll leave your rucksack by your jeep and call you later.' His words spilled from the moving car before disappearing into the distance. Not waiting for a response. Not offering her a lift. Simply leaving her in the barren landscape as the icy wind and rain chipped away at her frozen body.

Sobbing, numb, and feeling the grief of losing her mother all over again, Anna began to run the several miles that still lay between her and the old lodge. Running as fast as she could towards the lodge, her jeep, and away from the relative who couldn't have been more different to her mother.

CHAPTER ELEVEN

Anna's run slowed to a saunter. The crisp, blue sky of the morning had lost in its battle against turbulent clouds rolling in off the Atlantic. Roaring wind and pouring rain battered her frozen body, as sheep bleated their ambivalence. An empty barren landscape lay before her, too exposed for trees to thrive. Anna could see for miles.

The choppy North Atlantic Ocean reflected the turbulent sky above and splayed out in the distance, while the steep incline that led to The Old Lodge was dwarfed by the vastness of the rolling hillside.

Boulders left behind by glaciers dappled the landscape across Skye, and as Anna continued towards the lodge, she slumped onto one of the many that caused the track from the cottage to zigzag its way across the stunning landscape.

Wiping muck from her ruined dress boots, she cursed herself for leaving her winter jacket in her jeep and for choosing today, of all days, to dress up. As the damp chill continued to penetrate her layers, goosebumps gave way to shivers. At the same time, she was fighting to gather her hair that currently billowed to the tune of the blustery wind. The hairband often wrapped around her wrist for such moments quickly curtailed her blonde mass into an unruly bun.

Drawn to the ocean, she looked out at the vastness – calming, and a million miles from her life back in Edinburgh. And even now, after the morning she'd had and the discoveries she'd made, she still had no desire to return. At least not for any other reason than to collect her mother's desk. She was desperate to have it nestled in her cottage, on her own little patch of the island.

The revving of an engine in the distance wrenched her from her thoughts. It didn't sound like a car. She realised it was a quad bike just as the rider with the enticingly dreamy, moody brown eyes pulled up alongside her again.

He took a jacket from his lap and placed it on the boulder beside her, his gaze intense. His face, cool and expressionless, gave hints of a frown lurking beneath a woollen hat. 'Get on. I'll take you to your jeep.'

But his words were lost to the wind. She shivered. While his lack of expression rendered her speechless, his stare, piercing and intense, bore into her, just as it had earlier that morning.

'Okay, suit yourself.'

The engine revved as he drove off.

Zipping herself into the welcome warmth, Anna watched Hamish guide the quad bike off the track onto the barren landscape, disappearing from sight and reappearing as he expertly navigated the ups and downs of the undulating terrain.

Knowing she should have either asked him to repeat himself or plucked up the courage to ask for a lift, she left her perfectly placed boulder behind and continued down towards the lodge, all the while wondering if the earthy smell of the jacket belonged to Hamish.

Her face stung as the rain, now torrential, bit at her skin. The wind whipping in from a North Atlantic storm seemed determined to hamper her every step. Turning a sharp bend, the zigzagging track towards the rear of The Old Lodge came into view. On a landscape that was steep in places, the lodge looked small, lost in the vastness between them. Her heart sank at the realisation she still had a few miles to navigate.

Stopping to catch her breath, Anna took in the detail of the landscape. She could almost see where the land had been separated and sold off. Outbuildings, old and in dire need of repair, sat midway between her and The Old Lodge, and Anna presumed they still belonged to the lodge, going by the fencing that appeared to separate the croft from its neighbours.

The winds, becoming stronger, charged up the hillside, bombarding her with gravel and earth. The rain drove into her, soaking her to her core. Low cloud now skirted the hillside, hampering her view. Knowing she had to get to safety, she coerced her frozen legs into running.

Hoping for shelter, Anna ran towards the outbuildings rising precariously from the neglected ground, stumbling as she navigated potholes, half exposed stones, rocks, and rubble.

With her body drenched, she shivered, desperate for both warmth and consolation, as she stumbled towards the first of the doors. Its padlock was firmly in place, so she grappled with the second. The driving rain being thrust against her skin by the island wind continued to sting at her already battered cheeks. Rain, running down her neck, soaked her chest beneath the earthy jacket, while a constant stream ran from her forehead, catching in her eyelashes. Blinking the droplets away, she noticed the third padlock hanging limp. Coaxing her stiff, frozen fingers, she grappled with the lock until it fell to the ground. She tugged at the door, only to discover it slid sideways, and she managed to move it just enough to squeeze inside.

By the dim light of the open door, Anna could make out an old trailer and an assortment of troughs and hay racks scattered within a fenced-off area partitioned into rudimentary segments she presumed were sheep pens. There were also various tools, fence posts, and a mishmash of wire and wood.

But it was bales of hay piled high at the far side that caught Anna's attention. She wove her way through the cramped barn towards a lone straw bale that had become loose, partially spilling its contents to the ground. She clambered on top, pushing herself into its crevices in a desperate attempt for warmth.

Wind battling with the torrential rain battered against the building's fragile wooden shell, clattering against the sheeted roof above. There was no respite from the rain. The cold temperature had caused condensation on the inside of the roof and a relentless barrage of droplets now bombarded her already drenched body. But it was still a welcome relief. Patting her cheeks in a futile attempt to soothe her face, her soaked hands ached. Her fingertips stung in frozen pain. Pulling the earthy jacket to her chin, she listened as the wind gathered pace.

The barn creaked around her. The hay giving some protection from the freezing concrete floor beneath. Her thoughts turned to her wood burner at home, the log fire at The Water's Edge, and Andy's winter warming delicacies. Her eyes closed.

CHAPTER TWELVE

As her arthritic fingers cleared the untouched tea from the table, the unnerving churn in the pit of Sarah's stomach couldn't be ignored. The day she had feared for almost thirty years, the day she had prayed she would never see, had arrived.

Picturing him sitting at the end of the table, she was confused that he called himself Ben. But names didn't matter. Sarah had recognised him the minute she had opened her door to them yesterday. What confused her, though, was how he had come to be with Anna.

After placing the cups in the sink, she tidied away the biscuits and retreated to the living room. A large Welsh dresser dominated the rear wall. Pulling at a handle, a drawer creaked open at the only pace her aching hands would allow.

A leather-bound notebook, tied with ribbon to keep its contents in place, had sat untouched for as long as Sarah could remember. She removed it from its resting place and went to give the fire a stoke before adding more logs. Then lowering her frail hips into her armchair, Sarah pulled a blanket over her knees before placing the leather-bound notebook on her lap.

It was going to take time for Sarah to muster up the courage to open it, to look through its pages and take herself back to the time before her world fell apart. A time when her life was mapped out in front of her. A time when she was happy.

Her eyes blurred with tears. Faces from the past danced before her. Tall, handsome and the love of her life, Callum, had been a friend of her brother's. He had swept her off her feet, made her happy, and provided her with a home in a cottage near Dunvegan.

After a small ceremony, they had danced the hours away with friends in a local hotel bar before he had carried her over the threshold and into the life they had been excited to share together.

Callum had been Sarah's one true love. The months leading up to their wedding had been the happiest she'd had during her nine decades on this earth. And having saved herself, their wedding night was to be one she would never forget. Not only because he had made her feel more loved than she had ever thought possible, but because when he had kissed her goodbye the following morning to tend to his sheep, she was never to see him again.

A heart attack was to rob them of the life they should have had. The life she and Callum had so happily chosen only hours before.

Heartbroken, devastated, and overwhelmingly crippled by grief, Sarah had become bitter. She begrudged others their happiness. While at the same time, she begrudged herself a life, a future. Her guilt imprisoning her in solitude.

But Callum had left her a parting gift!

CHAPTER THIRTEEN

'Geez, you're just everywhere, aren't you?' Hamish scoffed, as he grabbed a couple of tools. 'You city folks never heard of closing the barn door behind you? Just make sure you close it when you leave.'

But as he put the tools into the back of his battered Land Rover, Anna's silence worried him. And with a quick glance, he realised she hadn't moved. 'Hey, you okay? Hey.' Fighting his way through the chaos of the barn, he ran towards her lifeless body.

He swooped her up in one swift action and carried her to the Land Rover, laying her across the back seat. He got in the driver's seat and thought about what to do next.

He couldn't take her to Sarah's; he'd sussed that much. Instead, as he set off from the barn, he turned down the hill, drove past the lodge, and headed on to Lochside.

Bringing his Land Rover to an abrupt halt, Hamish looked over his shoulder. Anna was still out cold. He got out and opened the back, grappling to get a steady hold of her limp body. He picked her up and headed towards the house.

Abigail, who must have seen him arrive from her writing room, opened her door just in time for Hamish to rush in.

'She's soaked through and frozen.'

'It's okay. Take her in there.' Abigail pointed towards the living room. 'Lay her on the sofa. I'll get blankets.'

Hamish placed her down gently then he removed her boots and the jacket he had loaned her earlier.

'How long has she been like this?'

'I'm not sure. I gave her my jacket a while ago. You need to get the rest of her wet clothes off her. She's soaked through and chilled.'

'You go put the kettle on. I'll see to her.'

Hamish stood in Abigail's kitchen and his heart raced. There weren't many people left on the island who he cared about. Certainly not the old crow up in the cottage. Sarah had gone out of her way to make his life hell since the minute he'd arrived on the island. He gave back as good as he got, which infuriated her even more. But he knew he couldn't leave Iain alone with her, not now, not at this stage in his life. Iain had suffered enough. As far as Hamish was concerned, Iain living out his final years alone with that old crow was simply not an option.

The kettle clicking, Hamish set about making Anna a mug of tea, adding a couple of teaspoons of sugar.

'Right, she's out of the wet clothes. I've put baggy joggers and a fleece on her. It's all I could manage. And covered her in blankets. Can you help me move the sofa a little closer to the wood burner?'

Moments later, Anna was as close to the heat as they dared.

'You see if you can rouse her to sip some tea,' Abigail instructed. 'I'm going to call Doctor Smyth.'

Hamish shook Anna's shoulder gently with one hand and tenderly removed strands of wet hair from her face with the other. She was just as beautiful now as she was the first time he'd set eyes on her – sitting in The Water's Edge, engrossed in her laptop, and laughing the most gorgeous laugh with the owners.

That had been a couple of years ago, and since then there had been fleeting glimpses of her. He would occasionally pass her on the road or see her at The Old Lodge or The Water's Edge. But she was a city girl, not the type he would usually go for, and yet she was never far from his thoughts.

But he had to step back. She was with that cocky little fella that had been sniffing around the lodge over the last year. He had to respect that. She was with someone else. He had missed his chance. Not that he'd given himself one, he scolded inwardly. He'd made no effort. But, then, a city girl was never going to be interested in him. He'd accepted that a long time ago.

'Doctor Smyth's on his way. We've done all the right things. We've to heat her up slowly. Did she drink anything?'

'I couldn't rouse her, but there's a hint of colour coming into her cheeks.'

'Thank goodness.' Abigail smiled. 'You keep an eye on her and I'll call Rob at The Water's Edge.'

'Wait, what, you know her?'

'Yeah, it's Anna, Anna MacLeod. She's a friend. A photographer. She comes and uses the jetty sometimes. We usually spend more time chatting, though, than she does taking pictures.' Abigail laughed. 'She'll be okay here.'

'Well, yeah, I know that. I just didn't realise you knew each other,' he replied as calmly as he could, the words *Anna MacLeod* still ringing in his ears. 'Do you know if she's related to any of the MacLeods on the island?'

'Yes, I'm not quite sure how though. Her mum was from here. Helena. But she moved to Edinburgh before Anna was born.'

'H-Helena?'

'Yeah, I'm sure that's what Anna said.'

Hamish fell silent.

* * *

AN HOUR LATER, DOCTOR SMYTH HAD BEEN AND GONE. ANNA had woken just enough to appease him, and after checking her over, he was happy enough to leave her in Abigail's care.

Abigail stepped into the kitchen.

'How is she?' Hamish's words were out the instant Abigail came in.

'She's going to be fine. We've just to let her sleep and the doc says she'll be right as rain once she's woken up properly. I've messaged Jamie. He's going to stop in at the hotel on his way home. They're going to give him some of their homemade broth.'

'Okay, do you mind if I stay for a bit?'

'Course not. I'll make us some tea. You look like you could use a cuppa.'

Taking a seat at the table, Hamish rubbed his face in his hands.

'You like her, don't you?'

'What? No.'

'Yes, you do. I know a man in love when I see one.' Abigail chuckled. 'And, anyway, I know you too well.'

'I'm not—'

'Hi, mate. How are you?' Jamie interrupted, placing an oversized container of freshly made broth on the table.

'Good, thanks, mate. You?' Hamish answered, relieved at

Jamie's impeccable timing. 'Well, I should go. Maybe message me later. Let me know how she is?'

'Of course.' Abigail nodded. 'You did the right thing earlier, bringing her here. Go and say bye. She might hear you.'

But unsure of what to say, Hamish simply glanced into the living room before seeing himself out.

CHAPTER FOURTEEN

Anna clambered out of Jamie's truck. 'Thanks, guys. I'll get your clothes back to you soon, Abi.'

'No rush. You just get yourself home and have a lazy day. I'll call you later. And remember, Rob's popping in to see you in an hour, so no dillydallying around here. That means your camera stays in your bag,' Abigail joked.

'Yeah, yeah.' Anna rolled her eyes. 'Seriously, though, thank you for everything.'

'It wasn't just us. It was Hamish who came to your rescue. You, eh, might want to catch him at some point.'

A cheeky wink accompanied Abigail's teasing smile.

Watching Jamie and Abigail drive off down the hill, Anna couldn't help but feel she would be the last person Hamish would want to see. But it reminded her of the message Hamish had sent Abigail earlier that morning to say he'd found her rucksack and had stashed it in a safe place around the back of the lodge. Anna set off to retrieve it from the old, metal delivery box she'd been told to look out for.

Having been panicked about her camera, Anna was relieved to find her rucksack dry. And retrieving her keys, she picked her way through the uneven ground in her dried-by-the-wood-burner, but ruined, boots.

On reaching the front of the lodge, the familiar sound of the quad bike closed in.

And failing in her attempts to reach her jeep in time, Anna noticed Hamish seemed just as uncomfortable at their meeting as she was.

Cutting his engine, he strode towards her. Taller, broader, and moodier than she remembered. His eyes boring into hers, just as they always did. Enticing, yet cold. Caring, yet distant. Anna felt herself flush, just as she'd done in the cottage the previous day.

Silence, always silence with him, she scoffed, before remembering her outfit. Still in Abigail's baggy jogging bottoms, fleece, and a jacket she had borrowed, Anna cringed when she remembered her entire ensemble was topped off with her ruined boots.

Not to mention that after showering at Abigail's, she had pulled her hair into a tight bun, had no make-up on, and was coughing and spluttering with the beginnings of a cold. Anna knew she was no vision.

'How are you feeling?' Hamish asked.

'I'm okay. Much better, thanks. I, eh, I'm sorry I caused so much hassle for you yesterday. And I just wanted to say thank you. I really appreciate what you did.'

'Yeah, well, anyone else would have done the same thing.'

'Maybe not. They might not have come back to check on me,' she said, wondering why he made her so nervous. 'Abigail told me what you did. Thank you.'

'Yeah, well, I see you got your rucksack.'

She nodded. 'I've no idea how it's dry. I thought it'd be ruined.'

'I rescued it from the rain. Thought that camera of yours

might be in there. That boyfriend of yours just left it by your jeep.'

'He's not my boyfriend,' she said. 'We've only just met.'

'Just met. Well, shit, isn't he a clever one? Taking up with you. Just watch him. I've a bad feeling about him.'

'I get the impression you've a bad feeling about most people,' she retorted, instantly regretting her comment.

'Oh, wow, not quite as charming as you look, are you?' Hamish replied.

And as she watched him get back on his quad bike and disappear into the distance, she couldn't help but wonder how her attempt at an apology had turned into a character assassination.

Back in her jeep, Anna started her engine and wondered what Hamish could possibly have against Ben. His comments reminded her about their encounter up at the cottage with Sarah – Hamish's expression when he'd looked at Ben and how it had changed when he'd looked at her.

Ben. He had been oddly quiet up in the cottage. And she wasn't sure what to make of that, given he'd never been stuck for words in the few days she'd known him. She'd found him to be quite the opposite: confident and not afraid to be forward. The more she thought about it, the more out of character it seemed. But as she thought about their meeting with Sarah and the discovery that she was her great-aunt, Anna thought that perhaps Ben had simply been politely allowing her to take the lead. It was, after all, her relative they had just discovered.

That conclusion led her back to Hamish. With no sign of a smile, personality, or iota of emotion, he had done something kind, and she had thrown it back in his face with her unnecessary and undeserved comment. After all, who was she to know how he would treat people? She didn't know him.

But what was his connection to the lodge, the cottage, and Sarah? He had wandered into the cottage as if he had every right to be there. Was he Sarah's grandson and, therefore, Anna's second cousin, or was he simply an employee? And what about her grandfather?

Anna was just realising all the questions she should have asked her great-aunt when she had the chance. But at the same time, too afraid of the answers, she was relieved she hadn't had the courage.

Movement in the corner of her eye alerted her to the quad bike. Hamish crossed the hill below The Old Lodge, a collie dog sitting obediently in the back, obviously used to being ferried around. Hamish appeared to know the ground well, swerving nature's obstacles while still zipping on. Suddenly, his brown eyes were all she could think about, reminding her again of how bad she felt for her nasty retort.

Remembering her jeep was loaded to the brim with the perfectly mounted and framed photographs she'd planned to deliver to the galleries, Anna began searching through her orders. Each gallery had its own designated bundle. Selections of the island's countryside, shoreline, and views over the open water, along with the animals, flora, and fauna that inhabited each landscape.

There were varying sizes. Some pieces were sizeable enough to be the centrepiece of a wall or focal point above a fireplace. Others, smaller, could be arranged in sets or hung as a stand-alone piece. Opening a small box that had been positioned perfectly to hold the larger pieces in place, Anna searched through gift cards she'd had printed from a selection of her best-selling photographs. They were becoming increasingly popular with tourists who wanted a keepsake but didn't have much luggage space.

She flicked through the neatly bundled cards until she found the image she was looking for. She pulled it out and laid the rest of the bundle aside, making a mental note to replace the card when she returned home.

Then, rummaging through her rucksack, she found a pen and closed her eyes, allowing her words to dance in her head until she had filtered out those needed to make her apology.

My attempt at an apology...

You unfairly bore the brunt of what has been an overwhelming couple of days. I'm sorry for snapping at you and I'm even more sorry if I upset you.

You heroically came to my rescue yesterday, and for that, I'm eternally grateful.

Thank you also for the thoughtful loan of your jacket. Maybe, one day, I could buy you a pint or dinner as a proper thank you.

Anna :)

CLOSING THE CARD, SHE RAN HER FINGERS ACROSS WHAT WAS her favourite of all the photographs she had taken on the island, The Old Lodge nestled against an autumnal backdrop.

She could still remember crouching down to find an angle that made the most of The Old Lodge's imposing front against the backdrop of the rolling hill and the sky above. Having arrived in time for sunrise, she had captured the dramatic sky in all its glory as shards of light showered the lodge in vibrant colours, illuminating its beauty while sheep lay scattered and resting on the encroaching land.

The original had hung in her living room for several years, enlarged, and in a frame big enough to ensure it was the focal point of the room. It was also the first image to greet anyone visiting her website, and a small print of the same picture sat in her bedroom in Edinburgh.

Lifting the lid of the deliveries box, she folded Hamish's jacket, placing it neatly with the card tucked into the collar just enough so it wouldn't fall off.

CHAPTER FIFTEEN

Having spent the previous few days at The Water's Edge with Rob and Andy, Anna had staved off her cold and was also feeling much better within herself. Early morning strolls along the harbourfront with Rob, helping Andy in the kitchen, and chatting with the locals had done her the power of good, reminding her that those she did have in her life were incredibly valuable.

And having returned to her cottage long enough to have a shower, blow-dry her hair, and apply some light make-up, Anna was feeling back to her old self.

Anna thought an hour or two with her camera would do her the world of good and had messaged Abigail to see if her jetty was free. It was, but Abigail had replied to say she had an appointment in Portree and wouldn't be back for a couple of hours. Deciding to go anyway, Anna drove across the island towards Dunvegan, only this time with no intention of going near The Old Lodge. In fact, she wasn't sure when or if she would be able to go back. Meeting Sarah had only served to distance her from the contents of her mother's box, the letter, and photographs.

The dirt track leading to Lochside was one Anna had driven often. Almost directly across from the track leading up to The Old Lodge, it led to a stunning shoreline and Abigail's home. Anna had gotten to know Abigail and Jamie quite well in recent years after initially approaching Abigail to ask if she could use the jetty occasionally to take photographs.

She now found she used it two or three times each season and had often spent an hour or so chatting on the jetty with Abigail after she had finished and packed away her camera and various lenses. Today, though, she wasn't sure whether she was relieved she would be alone or if she craved Abigail's company.

Pulling up at Lochside, Anna wrapped herself in her winter layers and set about arranging her tripod at the end of the jetty. But instead of attaching her camera, she lowered herself onto one of Abigail's chairs and allowed the cold North Atlantic winds to clear away the cobwebs.

She listened as the sea crashed against the legs of the jetty, sloshing beneath her in rhythmic waves. A power boat glinted in the sporadic winter sun as it made its way into the sea loch from the open water. Meanwhile, Abigail's resident heron seemed as ambivalent to her arrival as the sheep.

'A penny for them?'

Both startled and relieved at the sight of Abigail walking down the jetty with a Thermos cup in each hand, Anna gave her friend a hug.

'This isn't like you. You've normally taken a trillion pics by now.'

Abigail's concerned tone was evident.

'Thought you might like some hot chocolate.' She winked, handing Anna a cup and taking the seat beside her.

'Oh, wow, if ever there was a time to pitch up with hot chocolate, it's now. Thank you,' Anna gushed. 'Thought you were stuck in Portree?'

'I was, but I thought I'd switch things around and come

back early, see how you're doing. Do you want to talk about it, or would you rather we just enjoy the loch?'

'Talk about what?'

'The other day, your hair, outfit, face, which was still blotchy from crying, even though the rest of you was blue. Or we can just watch the ducks, if you'd rather. I'm feeling you might just need the company either way.'

'I'm not sure you'd believe me. It's like a plot from one of your books.'

'Try me.'

Turning to face her friend and clutching her cup as though it would give her the strength to discuss recent events, Anna began unburdening to her friend. 'Do you know Hamish, the guy who brought me here the other day?'

'Yeah, he's a good friend of ours. Jamie's known him for years.'

'Do you know his last name?'

'Eh, Mc-something, I think? I'd need to ask Jamie.'

'Don't bother Jamie with it,' Anna replied. The *Mc* part was all Anna had needed to hear.

'Why, is it him? That's upset you, I mean.'

'No, he's moody and obviously finds me a nuisance, but he did give me a loan of a jacket the other day before coming to my rescue.'

'So, who's upset you?'

After telling Abigail about her visits to the archive centre, and her chat with Mairead, Anna went on to recount her visit to the cottage with Ben, and her sadness at finding a great-aunt who was more concerned about ridding herself of her own guilt than asking how she was. 'I just ran. Abigail, it was quite pathetic. I'd so many questions and I didn't ask one. I'm no further forward now than I was before. And, if anything, it's worse because I've found a relative who–who was just horrible.

And finding someone so horrible has made me want to walk away. I'm no longer interested.'

The two sat in silence for a few minutes. Anna knew her friend well enough to know she would be mulling things over, deciding on the best way she could comfort Anna.

'Jamie's at the boatyard just now, but I'll ask him about the old man and your great-aunt when he gets back. He knows everyone, with his mum and dad owning the shop. I'll ask him about Hamish, too. But,' Abigail said, sipping at her hot chocolate, 'aren't you a little curious about Ben? I mean, he's come out of nowhere, and then he's just driven off and left you upset in the pouring rain. Have you heard from him since?'

Anna hadn't given Ben much thought since he'd driven off, other than him being unusually quiet in the cottage. She'd been too preoccupied. But as Abigail's words lingered, she realised his silence was unusual given how keen he had been to keep in touch beforehand. Her friend had a point!

As they chatted and dissected recent events, Abigail helped Anna to rationalise her feelings. Before long the two were laughing and joking, with Anna telling Abigail how mortified she'd been meeting Hamish at the lodge, wearing baggy jogging bottoms and ruined dress boots.

'I think he likes you.'

'What, who, Hamish?'

'Yup.'

'No, absolutely not. I'm a blot on his landscape, whenever I'm around him.'

'Oh, I don't think you are,' Abigail teased. 'You wait and see.'

CHAPTER SIXTEEN

Anna had managed to grab her favourite table at The Water's Edge between the fire and the bar and was tucking into another of Andy's delicious creations.

A couple of text messages between Anna and Rob seemed to have been enough to convince him that although she was more or less back to her old self, the situation with Ben was still preying on her mind.

Andy had responded by adding one of her favourites to the specials board and had made sure a portion was set aside for her. And as Anna tucked into chicken stroganoff with rice and a side order of roasted vegetables, she felt her concerns momentarily melting away.

The unexpected treat had been Rob coming to take her empty plate away, only to replace it with sticky toffee pudding, vanilla ice cream, and lashings of toffee sauce. And she was just scraping the dregs from her bowl when Ben wandered in, smiling as though it was just another day.

'Hey, how are you?'

Unsure of how to answer, Anna managed a shrug, her conversation with Abigail still fresh in her mind.

'I wasn't sure what to do the other morning. I felt like a bit of an intruder, like I'd no business being there while you discovered what you did.'

'Or you could have been a friend at a time when I needed one?'

'Yeah, I know. I'm sorry, it was pretty shitty of me.'

'You just drove off,' she scolded.

'Did you want me around? I felt like maybe you'd want to be alone.'

But rather than answer, she shrugged her shoulders again. Their awkward silence broke as Rob appeared to clear away Anna's empty dessert bowl, although she suspected it was more to make his feelings clear to Ben.

'So where were you when you were needed?'

'I-I was just apologising to Anna. I didn't realise. I thought she'd want to be alone.'

'Hmmm' was Rob's only response. But it was obvious to Anna that it'd had more of an impact than any barrage would have done.

'You ordering anything?' Rob asked.

Ben glanced at the specials board. 'Chicken stroganoff, please.'

'It's done.'

'The curry then, thanks.'

'Certainly, sir.' And with that Rob sashayed to the next table, where a family of four had just finished perusing the menu.

Both Anna and Ben overheard their order, and Anna had to stifle a chuckle when one ordered chicken stroganoff and Rob responded with 'Certainly, sir.'

The awkwardness continued for much of the evening, with Ben trying hard to be the perfect gent and Anna quietly concluding he wasn't. The whole situation had become bizarre, and as she watched him finish the last of his curry, she couldn't help but wonder how much longer he had left on the island. She remembered him saying he had taken a couple of weeks off work, and she was now desperately hoping that his two weeks were coming to an end.

'I'll go order us a couple of coffees,' Ben announced, rising from his seat and grabbing their empty glasses.

Anna managed a nod, and as Ben joined the queue at the bar, her attention turned to a couple of tourists who had just escaped the winter chill. Rob was doing his utmost to find them a table. It would be unusual to find The Water's Edge anything but full and Rob had become a master at making space for his customers.

She watched as Rob appeared with a small table before gathering a couple of spare chairs from around the restaurant, resulting in two delighted customers who were now filling Rob in on their stay on Skye and plans for their remaining few days.

It was a skill Anna had often admired in Rob. He had a natural ability to put people at ease, make them feel special, and the result was returning customers year on year and a deluge of Christmas cards from around the world.

And as she let her eyes roam this cosy Portree nook, she noted that the ratio between tourists and locals was pretty much even, all credit to the hard work of Rob and Andy. Jim, local and always seen hogging the same seat at the end of the bar, was in his usual attire, a yellow high-vis jacket that Anna had never seen him without. Having lost his wife a couple of years ago, he would often call in after work, have a warm, healthy dinner and a non-alcoholic beer before heading home.

Anna had often wondered if his visits were, given his choice of seat, as much for the company as the food. He definitely enjoyed the constant banter with Rob, Vinny their part-time barman, and whoever was standing in the queue.

Continuing her journey around the restaurant, she saw tonight's guests were mostly couples, apart from a group of holidaymakers, about a dozen, who took up the farthest corner with a wall of backpacks piled up behind. And a small group of men, similar in age to Anna, maybe a bit older, who appeared to be local. They had taken over a table near the bar, more often used by those who had just popped in for a few drinks.

She didn't recognise them until the one who'd had his back to her went to the bar for another round of drinks. He was familiar, but Anna couldn't for the life of her work out where she knew him from. Casually but smartly dressed in jeans and a shirt, the man returned to his table to find another had joined, causing them all to move around, making room for the late arrival. The guy in jeans and casual shirt was now sitting side-on.

Was there something familiar? She couldn't decide. Maybe his stubble. He was having a good laugh and was obviously funny, going by the reactions of the others when he spoke. And the more he laughed, the more she decided she didn't know him.

Ben returning with their coffees interrupted her thoughts.

'Sorry I've been a while. Rob had a go at me for *abandoning* you, as he put it, the other day. That wasn't my intention. I just felt like I was intruding, that it was your moment.'

Anna was becoming annoyed with his complete lack of empathy. He constantly spoke as though he had been thinking of her, but in fact, he kept making it about himself and what he was thinking. 'Look, you just drove off in the pouring rain and howling wind. There's quite a few miles between the cottage and the lodge and you just left me, in horrendous weather with no coat. I was already soaked through when you saw me. Do you realise the state I ended up in? But, you know, you don't really know me. You don't owe me anything. So just forget it.' She knew her annoyance with him would be obvious for all to see.

And finding it hard to look at Ben, she looked beyond to the table she'd spotted earlier. But this time, the man who had been so familiar to her was now looking directly at her. His seductive yet moody brown eyes stared directly at hers. His laughter had stopped, his expression serious.

Initially, feeling annoyance at his stare, her eyes bore back at his. But the more she absorbed his expression, which was without the woolly hat that would ordinarily accentuate his mood perfectly, the more she realised he appeared worried. His wrinkled brow, that she had seen a hint of previously, was soft and concerned. His eyes not leaving hers, she knew he had just witnessed her crossed words with Ben.

His expression unchanging, his eyes settled on her as if reiterating his presence. Anna felt unusually safe. Like she wasn't alone, not that she was ever alone in The Water's Edge with Rob and Andy. But for a fleeting moment, she felt his moody stare had her back.

'I'm sorry. I really am. Can we start over?' Ben pleaded, playfully. 'Here, I got us a bag of crisps to share with our coffee.' Opening the pack so they could both pick away at them easily, he placed the bag between them.

'Thank you,' Anna said before looking back at Hamish. But his attention had returned to his friends.

CHAPTER SEVENTEEN

Having finally delivered her prints to the galleries on the mainland, Anna was almost home when she decided a well-deserved stop at Brother's Point was in order. Just a few miles from her cottage, the headland jutted out into the straights separating Skye and Raasay. Anna would often venture down the sharp incline to the jagged rocks and grassy slopes.

Pulling into a lay-by at the side of the road, she changed into her walking boots, pulled her hair into a tight bun, and piled on her layers. The walk down to Brother's Point was steep but one she loved. And after waving to the local crofter as he tended his sheep and stopping to speak to a couple of locals, Anna found herself walking across footprints left by dinosaurs millions of years before.

Like most locals, she could point out most of the footprints, but she loved watching tourists hunt for them, especially children. They were always full of hope as they inspected the rocks beneath their feet, but excitement often reached fever pitch when footprints were spotted. And once the tourist knew what they were looking for, they quickly began spotting others.

Sometimes she would get chatting to parents, and if they

had been searching unsuccessfully for a while, she would join in, leading their children to the footprints in a way that made them think they'd found them themselves.

To Anna, it was always a cheerful place. A camaraderie often sparked between strangers as they united in their search for the prehistoric imprints. Today, though, it was quiet, probably down to the lateness in the day. But with only an hour or two of daylight left, Anna knew the softness of the light against the backdrop of the ocean would be stunning, and the hope of the next great shot was never far from her thoughts.

As she continued down the steep slope, the bleating sheep and circling gulls intermingled with the sound of the ocean was enough to bring her to a stop. Breathing in the fresh air, taking in the beauty, she wished she had more time to wander through the ruins and out to the farthest point of the headland. But it was the incoming waves crashing against the rocks that Anna was hoping to capture today.

The cold, blue sky, pebble dashed with grey, reflected on the Atlantic Ocean below. The encroaching waves roared, thundered, as the force of the ocean smashed them against the rocks, only for them to break into stunning displays of white spray that rose metres into the air.

Crouching down, Anna caught the rising waves from ground level. Stunning, beautiful, and dramatic. The late afternoon light was soft and glorious, forming the perfect backdrop to the ocean's exquisite display. And as her camera continued to click, her lens zooming in and out, she knew the universe had aligned and she had a stunning new collection in the making – her finger, holding for continuous clicks, ensuring she caught nature at its very best.

Capturing an array of photographs from several vantage points, Anna made the most of her time before the fading light forced her to pack away her camera. And just as she was about to begin her ascent back up the hill, Anna noticed a man standing a few metres away.

Used to meeting tourists and locals alike at Brother's Point, she would normally say hello and continue her walk. But there was something about him that unsettled her. Dressed from head to foot in black, with a scarf obscuring much of his face, he wasn't looking out to the ocean or searching the ground for dinosaur footprints. His eyes were most definitely fixed on her.

A quick check and Anna could see a dog walker in the distance making his way towards them from the headland. As she went about her days photographing the island, she often forgot her camera, lenses, and accessories were worth a small fortune. She decided the best thing to do would be to walk towards the dog walker. She could then make her way back up the hill towards her car, remaining in his sight until she was far enough ahead.

The path leading up towards the main road snaked its way around the hillside and Anna could see easily that the man in black appeared determined to keep up with her. However, scrambling up hills was something she had mastered. She'd had plenty of practice as many of her favourite locations on the island usually involved a climb at some stage.

Keeping an eye out for the dog walker, Anna continued her climb. There was no sign of the crofter from earlier, and the time of day meant there was no one else beginning their descent to the point. All she could do was keep going.

Reaching the main road, she ran towards her jeep, jumping in just in time to see the man in black appearing a few yards behind her. Standing as if struggling to catch his breath, he turned the other way, giving the impression he was taking in the views and the sea in the distance. But not before Anna got a full glimpse of his face. She recognised him instantly as the man Ben seemed to quietly acknowledge entering The Water's Edge a few nights before.

Leaving the lay-by behind, Anna manoeuvred her jeep passed an old blue hatchback. Dented on the driver's side, it was filthy and splattered with mud. Presuming it belonged to the man still looking out to sea, she craned to take a mental note of the number plate, before driving off. Though it was obscured by mud, she decided it possibly started with *SV*, but she couldn't be sure.

Anna drove the remaining few short miles into Staffin, regularly checking her rear-view mirror. The last thing she wanted to do was lead him directly to her door. But there had been no sign of him since she'd left the car park. And turning onto her little patch of the island, she continued around to the rear of her cottage, parking her distinctive jeep out of sight of the main road for the second time in a week.

* * *

WHILE THE IMAGES FROM BROTHER'S POINT UPLOADED TO HER PC, Anna put the kettle on and lit the wood burner. A bung-in-the-oven cottage pie was lurking in her fridge and she had a bottle of red calling her name.

After changing into a pair of leggings and comfy sweatshirt, she pulled her brush through her hair. And catching herself in the mirror, she realised she was looking more like her old self. Time away from Ben and the lodge had been good for her, she decided. And with that, she pulled her hair into a neat ponytail.

She loved an evening at The Water's Edge with Rob and Andy, but curling up on the sofa with dinner while the heat from the wood burner enveloped her body was just what she needed.

Having caught up with her connections at the galleries in the morning, she'd had a few unexpected orders after a flurry of end-of-season tourists had made their purchases. Many galleries had shut their doors for the winter, but a select few in the less remote areas stayed open out of season and were preparing for the tourists who flocked to the island year-round. They opened fewer hours and were usually close to the larger hotels that accommodated coachloads of tourists as they passed through. But despite these coaches bringing fewer tourists during the winter months, especially over Christmas and New Year, Anna was often surprised at how many of her images sold in the quieter months.

Convinced she had captured some fantastic images at Brother's Point, she decided that tomorrow would be a cosy day at home. She would work her way through the images and hopefully find she had the beginnings of a brand-new collection for next year.

Anna retrieved her cottage pie from the oven. She poured herself a glass of red and settled on the sofa. Her thoughts turned quickly to the man at Brother's Point. But she soon decided she had been paranoid. Had the shoe been on the other foot, she might have watched a photographer as they crouched on the rocks getting into all sorts of odd positions in the hope of capturing the perfect image. She probably would have found it quite amusing.

CHAPTER EIGHTEEN

Waking early the following morning, Anna's eagerness to begin working on her images from Brother's Point staved off any thoughts of a long lie-in. Up, showered, dressed, and munching her way through toast by just gone eight, Anna waited for her PC to spring to life.

Wishing she had her mother's desk for such moments, she knew that perhaps a trip to Edinburgh might be needed in the coming weeks, a thought that was quickly quashed as the first of several hundred images began appearing on screen.

Anna knew instantly she had enough for a full collection. A few weeks of sifting through, discarding the ones that were immediately no good, before separating and editing the perfect images from the *maybes* – the thought of having such an exciting project to work on over the winter months filled her with excitement.

The morning passed in a flash with Anna lost in the sheer enjoyment of her images. She had made a start, discarding more images than she had kept. But that was the norm. It was the clear, crisp gems that she was looking for. The ones that flawlessly captured nature and the island in all their extraordinary glory.

She was just stopping for lunch when there was a knock at her door. Presuming it was Mrs Stewart with a fresh supply of eggs, Anna answered her door with a beaming smile.

But she felt her expression change dramatically as she encountered Hamish standing there, as expressionless as ever. His collie dog leaned out of the window of the old Land Rover as if whatever exchange was about to take place was going to be pure gold.

He kept up the persona of a man of few words, his silence awkward as Anna tried to comprehend why he would be knocking on her door.

His stubble led once again to the hint of a frown lurking below his woollen hat. Although, Anna decided, having seen him in The Water's Edge, it was possibly more of a concerned frown than the annoyed grimace she'd always presumed was hidden beneath the layer of wool. 'Hi,' she managed.

'Hi. I, eh, I just came to check you were okay.' He looked everywhere but at Anna. 'You haven't been back at the lodge, and after the other day, I wanted to check you hadn't come down with the flu or something?'

'I'm fine. I just haven't wanted to go back.' She sighed, wondering exactly how much he knew. Had Sarah filled him in on her visit with Ben? Had she sent him? Absolutely not. She scolded herself for even thinking that Sarah might have the slightest interest in her wellbeing. Meaning it was more likely Hamish was asking out of genuine concern. 'Thank you, though, for asking.'

'Okay, well,' he said, turning to leave, 'just don't let that old crow stop you in whatever interest you have in the place.'

'Old crow. Isn't she your grandmother?'

'Good lord, no.'

Now *that* was a frown of annoyance, Anna decided. 'So, what's your connection, if you don't mind me asking?'

'I just work for the old man. I put up with her to make sure he's okay.' He paced back in the direction of the collie.

Anna watched as, head bowed, he got into the Land Rover and started the engine. He was just driving off when he stopped, opening his window.

'There was another reason I came. There was a man at the lodge yesterday, asking if I knew you. He was the shifty kind, a bit like that Ben. I said I didn't, but when you hadn't been back at the lodge, I just thought I'd better check on you.'

His window closed and Anna ran out, signalling for him to open it again. 'Was he dressed from head to toe in black? I don't know his hair colour as he was wearing a hat when I saw him.'

'Yeah. He was wearing black trousers and a black jacket.'

Anna nodded. Perhaps her first instincts about the man at Brother's Point had been correct.

'You know him?'

'No, but was he driving an old blue hatchback, dented at the front?'

'Yeah, that's him.'

Anna didn't go into the details of the previous day, but the fact the mystery man had been at The Old Lodge had to be more than a coincidence. After all, the lodge wasn't exactly a tourist spot.

'Just be careful.'

'Wait, why don't you like Ben?'

'Do you?'

'I don't know him.'

His frown returned.

'I don't. I photograph The Old Lodge because I love it. There's something about being there…I can't explain it. That's where I saw Ben. I-I think my mum has connections to it, well I know she does, since—'

'Since your chat with the old crow?'

'Yeah, she's something else.' Anna rubbed her arms to stave off the chill. 'And now, what was my favourite place on the island is a place I'm not sure I'll ever be able to go back to.'

His moody brown eyes softened. Anna was once again taken aback by her feelings. Was Hamish genuine in his apparent concern for her? Or was he simply making sure the annoying pest who kept trespassing and getting into bother was alright? She wasn't sure, but what she did realise was she felt safe when he was around.

'Right, well, just be careful.'

Hamish's features melted into the expressionless stare she was more used to.

'But wait, why don't you like Ben?'

'You'd have to ask him.'

CHAPTER NINETEEN

Ben was just pulling up at their Airbnb on the outskirts of Portree when Dylan arrived in the puff of black smoke that typically accompanied his old, dented hatchback.

'I've picked us up something for dinner,' Dylan announced, waving two pizza boxes towards Ben.

'Not margherita again?'

'Stop complaining. I'm not paying for it, so it's whatever's by the door. And, anyway, I'm feeding you, aren't I? You want something better, then you go nick tomorrow night's tea.'

Having discarded the empty boxes beside the others from the previous evenings, Ben put the pizzas in the oven while Dylan made one of his many phone calls. 'Never any money for food,' Ben muttered under his breath. 'But he's always topping up that bloody phone.'

Dylan ending his call and throwing his phone on the table was enough to warn Ben he was in for a rough night.

'We need to get this show on the road,' Dylan announced impatiently. 'You still got no idea where the fucking thing is?'

'No, I can't just ask her outright.'

'Come on, you've had days. How useless do you need to be, for fuck's sake!'

'What do you expect me to do? Just come out with it? *Anna, can you tell me where I can find the painting that my crooked twin thinks is worth at least a hundred grand?* I don't even think she knows. She'd never been in the lodge, hasn't had anything to do with the family. I mean, how the hell will she know where it is?'

'Don't you talk to me like that.' Dylan grabbed him by the scruff of the neck and rammed him against the wall. 'I think you're forgetting the urgency here,' he said, his face inches from Ben's. 'If we get our hands on that painting, my debts are cleared. Do you hear me? They're wiped clean.' Letting Ben go, he paced the floor. 'Do you know how many years I've been owing that scum?'

Ben shook his head.

'Too many.' His temper flared again. 'Too damned many, and now I have the chance to have that debt wiped clean. Wiped clean, do you hear me?' His fist ricocheted off the table with enough force to send his mobile phone flying. 'If we can't get our hands on it, I'll have no hands left to be swiping you pizzas or anything else for that matter. They've given me one more week to come up with some way of settling my debts, and that painting is my only chance. You hear me? Do you hear me?' he roared. Loud enough and close enough for Ben to feel the spit on his face. 'And anyway,' he said with an unnerving calmness accompanied by an expression Ben couldn't quite decipher, 'there's possibly far more for us here than just an old painting.'

CHAPTER TWENTY

The following morning, Anna was keen to speak to Ben, and at just coming up for eleven, she messaged to ask if he would meet her at The Water's Edge at twelve. That would give her enough time to call in to the archive centre for a quick chat with Crissie beforehand.

She'd decided there was more to Ben than he was letting on, so some quiet digging of her own was in order. And as one winter month rolled into the next, Anna found herself adding extra layers as she prepared to venture out into the island weather.

Sheep sashaying across the road at their leisure had been her only hold-up on the way to the archive centre. But she had cause to pause again when, pulling into a parking space, she spotted Ben approaching the archive door.

Anna knew she had to give him the benefit of the doubt. It was entirely plausible that he was hoping to clarify a few thoughts with Crissie before discussing them with her later. She had to give him a chance. Having made that decision, she about-turned and left the car park.

Not that her time would be wasted. The moody weather

that had brought with it a drop in temperature meant the harbour and views out to the Sound of Raasay would be stunningly atmospheric.

She made her way through town towards the Portree Trail. With her destination in mind, she parked by the shore and followed the footpath until she reached the boathouse and slipway.

The tide was out, meaning she could venture out to the farthest end of the slipway, giving her a clear view of the harbour, with its row of white, pink, yellow, and blue buildings that encompassed The Water's Edge.

Sailing boats tethered to buoys filled the foreground, while clouds rolling off the hills on the other side of the bay allowed shards of sunlight to break through, shimmering and dancing as they pierced the waves beneath.

Zooming in and out, she allowed her camera to capture the surrounding beauty. A shot of a sailing boat returning from the Sound of Raasay, its wake following on behind, was an image Anna was keen to see in full on her PC. Continuing around, she zoomed in on the harbour, just enough to see Ben's car pulling up across from The Water's Edge. Realising the time, she made her way back to her car.

As she headed for the harbour, she pondered Ben's earlier visit to the archive centre and decided not to mention it. After all, it was Abigail and Hamish who were suspicious of him, not her. So far, she had been able to rationalise his behaviour. But, as she pulled up outside The Water's Edge, she realised that rationalising his behaviour was something she was having to do all too often.

Finding Rob behind the bar, she gave him a hug before going into the kitchen to see Andy. Both men were deep in lunch preparation, but both were thrilled to see her. And with Andy promising to bring them something extra special for lunch, she went to find Ben.

A disapproving nod from Rob alerted her to where Ben was seated. Unusually, he had taken a seat by the window. Anna much preferred to be closer to the bar. It allowed for far more interaction from Rob and Andy.

'Hey,' Ben said, getting to his feet. 'How are you?'

'Fine, thanks.' Anna de-layered, hanging her coat and fleece on a neighbouring chair just in time for Rob to appear with two coffees.

Ben finally broke the silence. 'What have you been up to the last couple of days?'

'Photo editing, mostly. I wasn't sure if you'd still be on the island. You've gone quite quiet since our visit to the cottage.'

'Well, it's obvious there's no family there for me to find. So, I guess, I'm at a loose end.'

'Have you been back to the archive centre? See if Crissie can help?' Anna asked, cringing that she'd broken her resolution so early.

'Yeah, I nipped in before I came here, but she wasn't keen to talk. It just would have been great to find out a bit more about my mum's side.'

'Then why don't we call Mairead? I have her number somewhere.' Anna began searching through her rucksack for her notepad from the other day.

'No, it's okay. Probably not much point.'

'Right, okay, I know we don't really know each other, but I think it's only fair you're honest with me.'

'What do you mean?'

'I mean, you tell me the truth about why you're really here.'

'What? I have.'

'You've completely changed since we spoke to Sarah. What did she say that's scared you off? Why were you so desperate to drive away that you left me in the pouring rain? And why haven't you told me about whatever it is that's happened between you and Hamish? You're not getting any more information from me until you tell me what's really going on.'

'Nothing's going on, she didn't say anything, and I don't know what you're talking about with Hamish.'

'When did you first visit The Old Lodge?'

'Just last week. I told you. I'd only been here a day when I saw you there.'

'Okay, so why did Hamish refer to speaking to you last year?'

Ben blushed scarlet just as Andy brought them each a burger in a ciabatta bun with cheese and relish dripping down the sides, and a side of fries.

A quick chat with Andy may have broken the moment, but Anna wasn't letting Ben get away with not answering her question. 'So,' she prompted, once Andy left, 'the truth.'

Watching Ben squirm as she tucked into her burger, Anna knew too much had happened for her to let her question go. It was completely out of character for her, but she knew she had to stay strong.

'I've said before that I didn't have an easy childhood. I just want to know more, for my mum's sake.'

'Why, when she refuses to speak about her past? Doesn't that make you think that she doesn't want her past dragged up? And you still haven't answered my question. What is it with you and Hamish? Why are you hiding the fact you were at the lodge a year ago?'

His cutlery landed on the table loud enough for others to stare. 'I was at the lodge a year ago, but I was only passing as I was here with work. I stopped by for a few minutes and decided that I'd come back at some point. This is some point.' He shrugged his shoulders. 'I swear, I've nothing to hide. I had hoped we could be friends.'

'So had I, but I need to know I can trust you. And up until a few days ago, the thought that I couldn't hadn't entered my mind.'

His focus returned to his burger. 'You can trust me.'

'Have you got any idea what happened to me after you drove away and left me in the pouring rain and howling wind?'

He shook his head. 'No, you haven't told me.'

CHAPTER TWENTY-ONE

Driving towards Dunvegan, Anna dissected her conversation with Ben. It was entirely possible he was being honest with her. If his nature was to be laid-back, there was every possibility he didn't think facts were a big deal. But that side of him would be in stark contrast to the guy who, up until a few days ago, had been zipping around with a piece of paper in hand.

Not to mention that the laid-back theory would also be easier to believe had there not been such a change in him since meeting Sarah. Up until then, he had been attentive, caring, and friendly. He had given Anna the impression that, when it came to looking into their pasts, they were in it together. Now, she only heard from him if she instigated it.

After driving through Dunvegan, she continued towards Lochside and The Old Lodge. The tide was now coming in. The dreich sky low and imposing, it was a day that might have been better spent hunkering down by the wood burner while she drank hot chocolate and edited the photographs she had taken at Brother's Point. Instead, she knew she had to get to the bottom of whatever was going on, and if Ben wasn't prepared to give her an honest answer, then there was someone else who might.

Turning off the main road, Anna took a deep breath as she continued past The Old Lodge to the outbuildings that sat nestled in the hill between the lodge and the cottage. There was no sign of Hamish's Land Rover, but she wondered if he would be out on his quad bike. Hoping he might be out doing final checks before it got dark, she decided to hang around. Given she wasn't prepared to pay the old crow another visit, she had no idea how else to find him.

In no mood to photograph The Old Lodge or the surrounding area, Anna turned off her engine and waited. After attempting and failing to read a few pages of her book, she passed five minutes by eating a bar of chocolate conveniently stashed in her glove compartment. Scrolling through social media was just as boring – if not more so – than sitting waiting, and so she decided that watching the sheep graze a few feet from her jeep was by far the best way of passing the time.

As daylight began to fade, she started her engine and put her lights on. They had only been on a few minutes when Hamish's familiar Land Rover came into view. Parking along-side her, he opened his window.

'What are you doing here?'

His tone was softer than normal, his stare just as intense.

Odd, she thought, but his expression and tone didn't matter. Or the frown that constantly seemed to crumple his forehead, his eyes – moody, brown, and delicious – always seeming to bore into hers as though they desired her full attention.

Silence, as his stare intensified.

'I was hoping to speak to you.'

'How long have you been here?'

'A couple of hours.'

'Well, lucky you put your lights on, or I'd never have seen you.'

Shrugging, she said, 'I didn't know how else to find you.'

'I'd have thought you'd have asked Abigail.'

'I didn't know she knew you well enough to know where you stayed.'

'Follow me. You must be freezing, and anyway, the old crow at the top of the hill will see the lights. Best we go now before she decides to get her binoculars out.'

With that, he drove off, leaving Anna to follow.

About a mile up from the entrance to the lodge, another track led to an old cottage. Anna pulled up and turned off her engine. The cottage was traditionally white and similar in size to Anna's; it was surprisingly neat on the outside. A log store, far better stocked than her own, reminded her it was about time she placed another order.

A decked area to the side made the most of the views. Smoke belching from the chimney added to the cottage's appeal. And, as was to be expected, sheep dappled the surrounding landscape.

Noticing Hamish was already making his way towards the door, Anna grabbed her rucksack and followed.

A faint smell of something delicious mingling with the embers of the open fire met Anna before she was through the door. Like many converted bothies on the island, his cottage wasn't dissimilar to hers. Although, she was sure she was in the minority with her spiral staircase and converted loft.

Hamish took her coat and hung it by the door, before leading Anna into the living area. Surprisingly tidy, there were elements of a bachelor pad intertwined with homely accessories. A guitar rested on a stand beside a bookcase crammed full of Lee Child, Harlan Coben, and James Paterson novels, all sitting neatly in series.

'I thought you had a dog?'

'She stays with…Eh, she stays up at the cottage.'

'You can say her name, you know.'

Anna continued her wander around his living room. Blues, she decided, he liked blues. His sofa, rug, and curtains were all in keeping with the theme, set off against a stone wall that had been left untouched with an open fireplace, the remaining walls off-white.

Unlike hers, there was no breakfast bar, but a round table partitioned the two areas nicely. His kitchen, though obviously quite new, had a more traditional feel.

'Tea, coffee?'

'Tea, please,' Anna said, taking a seat at the table while Hamish busied himself with the kettle.

Indeed, a man of few words, Anna thought to herself as she wondered how to ease the polite yet uncomfortable atmosphere between them.

'You don't really like me, do you?'

Shit, her words were out before she'd had time to register the thought.

Hamish dropped the kettle lid. The silence that followed was enough to let Anna know that whatever his problem was, she'd just made it a hundred times worse.

'I'm sorry. I shouldn't have said that. It's just I'm not sure what I've done. But I'm nice, and friendly, and extremely grateful to you for coming to my rescue the other day.'

'Abigail saw to you. It's her you should thank.'

'She did, and I have. But if it weren't for you, I'd have still been lying frozen in that barn.'

'Milk? Sugar?'

'Just milk, please.'

Placing two mugs on the table, Hamish took the seat opposite Anna, his intense gaze firmly fixed on his tea.

'Thank you.' Anna sipped, grateful for the distraction.

'I don't dislike you. I don't know you.'

It was Anna's turn to shrug. 'There's plenty people that don't know me, but they don't look at me the way you do.'

Cringing at her second dose of verbal diarrhoea in as many minutes, Anna couldn't help but wonder what it was about him that made her speak her mind. It was as though she had lost all train of thought and the filter between her brain and mouth was non-existent. 'I'm sorry. I'm nervous, I guess. It's been a strange week and, well, to be honest, quite overwhelming.'

But normality resumed when Hamish's stare left the confines of his mug. The pool of brown that consistently melted so intensely into her once again had her rooted to the spot. Piercing and intense, yet enticing. Encased in the frown that she so often glimpsed beneath his hats.

And looking more closely, absorbing his features properly for the first time, Anna decided his frown was again one of concern. But was his concern for himself, the lodge, or her? Annoyed at herself for being unusually sceptical, she momentarily blamed Ben and the events of recent days.

But deep down, she knew things had gone too far, too much had happened, and whether she liked it or not, she had no option but to get to the bottom of what was going on. Knowing the stranger at Brother's Point had also been asking about her at the lodge had been the turning point. Now, there was no going back.

Still on the receiving end of Hamish's silence, she realised she was going to have to work at getting him on-side. For some reason, he was wary of her. Didn't trust her, which confused Anna, as she was one of the most loyal and trustworthy people she knew. Her only hope of moving forward with him, of uncovering the issues he seemed to have with her, was for her to get him on-side. And that, she decided, was going to take work.

There was no time like the present. 'Thank you for the tea. I was needing something hot. Aren't you drinking yours?'

Hamish rose from his chair. A nod of his head signalled to Anna to follow. Confused, she couldn't decide whether she was to follow mug-in-hand or leave it on the table. Surely her comment about his tea hadn't been so insulting that she was to leave?

But his expressionless stare was obviously more in tune with her thoughts than she was with his.

'Bring it with you. We'll sit by the fire if you're cold.'

Joining him on the sofa, Anna wondered how such an act of kindness could accompany *that* stare. His expressionless persona was an enigma she seemed destined never to decipher. But there was a reason he kept appearing in her life. She knew she needed to break the ice with him; she needed to garner his trust.

'Thank you.' Anna placed her mug on the coffee table and realised how small she must look next to him. He had to be over six feet and was well-built and muscled, as though he was used to manual labour and could take on the world. 'Maybe we should start again? I'm Anna, Anna MacLeod.'

'Hamish McPherson.'

'Mc-McPherson. You're not a MacLeod?'

'No.' Hamish shrugged.

'Oh, so you're working here by choice, not because they're your family?'

Hamish began rubbing his forehead, leading Anna to assume she had managed to offend him again.

'I'm sorry. I guess I just assumed. The way you just wandered into the cottage the other day. I thought you lived there.'

'Ah.' He sighed. 'That's why you thought the old crow was my grandmother.'

'Yeah, I'm sorry.'

'I'm here because I need to be here.'

His frown fell away, leading Anna to wonder if perhaps she was making progress. Although his reply was still as clear as mud.

'What does that mean?'

'It means I need to be here, at least for the next while.'

'Okay, so if you won't tell me why you're here, can you tell me why I get the feeling you know things that could help me?'

She watched as Hamish leaned forward, elbows on his knees, staring into the fire. He was noticeably uncomfortable, reluctant to speak. The flickering of the fire enhanced his features. He was strong, unnervingly attractive, and broodingly quiet. 'Maybe this is a bad idea. Maybe I should just go. Thank you for the tea.'

She got to her feet and was reaching for her coat when Hamish began to speak again.

'I'm not meaning to be awkward. I just need to be here just now, working here. When the time's right, I'll be able to move on.'

'That's all I want, to be able to move on. Not physically – I love the island, my cottage, and thank god I've got Rob and Andy,' Anna replied. 'But I need closure. I need to find out what The Old Lodge has to do with my mum, before I can even begin to move on with my own life.'

'And what about, what about…him?'

'Ben? You really don't like him, do you?' Anna retook her seat on the sofa.

'No,' he said, turning to face her. 'I really don't.'

His eyes were still just as piercing, just as enticing, and his expression remained indecipherable.

'Why?'

'Why does it matter to you?'

Anna jumped to her feet. 'That's it. I mean, what the hell! You're impossible. You're incapable of having an actual conversation. Why are you always so defensive? Why do you always stare at me? Are we supposed to know each other, or have you just decided I'm trouble and in cahoots with a man you obviously can't stand? Who, for the record, I'm not all that keen on either. But, forgive me'—she glared at him—'given the situation, he's all I've got.' She wiped tears from her cheeks. 'Don't you get it? I need him. He has links to my mum's past. I need him if I'm going to stand any chance of discovering the truth about my mum and what happened here. If I ever want to feel like I belong on this bloody lonely planet, then I need to find that link to my past.'

She fought to release her words through tears. 'I have no option but to put up with Ben and whatever it is that he's up to with that damn piece of paper of his.' With her arms flailing, she was mortified at the state she was in but determined to say her piece. 'So, the last thing I need is you going out of your way to be bloody awkward.'

His arms pulled her in, the earthy smell she recognised from his jacket engulfing her nostrils. He held her close. The overwhelmingly stressful events of the previous few days released onto the chest of a man who, despite everything else, had a way of making her feel as though she could be her true self. She didn't have to hide her emotions, hide her feelings, or her fears. She could be honest with the man she didn't know.

His hold was firm; strong but tender. He stroked her hair, wiping loose strands from her tears as they lay against the dampness of her cheeks. He caressed her back, until her involuntary sobs eased to the occasional sniff.

And all the while, she kept her eyes closed, lost in the moment, willing him never to let her go. Feeling his warmth, listening to the rhythmic beating of his chest – it had been years since she'd felt so alive. Felt so safe. Yet so many questions were left unanswered.

'Are you hungry? I have homemade soup and crusty bread, if you want some. Let you catch your breath, get some goodness in you, and then I'll answer your questions, I promise.'

Reluctant to peel her damp face from his chest, she felt herself nod.

'Okay, then, bathroom's along the hall. You can't miss it. You go…do whatever. Splash some cold water on your face or blow your nose.' He chuckled.

'Wow, a joke,' she croaked as she went in search of the bathroom.

Small, functional, and clean, she decided. Nothing to make it homely, other than a couple of towels on a rail. Everything else, she presumed, was hidden away in the vanity unit under the sink.

Dabbing her eyes, she removed her smudged mascara before flushing the toilet so Hamish wouldn't hear her blow her nose. What a sight, she cringed, before running her fingers through her hair.

But fixing her parting and untangling the damp strands that had been stuck to her face was enough to make her at least semi-presentable, she decided, having no option but to ignore her blotchy eyes and red nose.

By the time she was back in the kitchen, Hamish had set out their cutlery. A large loaf, the type she recognised from the artisan bakery in Portree, sat on a chunky chopping board in the centre of the table, butter sitting alongside.

'It smells delicious,' she managed.

'Thanks, it's just vegetable, but it'll do you good.'

'You made it yourself,' she said, trying desperately to make it sound more of an observation than a question.

'Yeah, you don't get long into your first winter on the island without learning how to make soup. Or cook, for that matter.'

Anna raised her eyebrows.

'What, you don't cook?'

'Don't, can't, it's a much of a muchness. But I've been spoiled a bit in that department. I go and see Rob and Andy at The Water's Edge.'

'Yeah, I'd sussed you know them well.'

'They were good friends of my mum's. But they're like

family, and pretty much all I have left.' Noticing Hamish's expression soften, she added, 'We used to stay with them when we visited the island.'

'You used to visit the island?'

'Yeah, most years.' Her attention waned as Hamish placed two bowls of hot deliciousness on the table.

'Right, tuck in,' he said, carving a few slices of bread.

Blowing gently on her first spoonful, Anna felt her eyes close. It had been a long time since she'd had soup that hadn't fallen from a can.

'So, what do you want to know?' Hamish downed his spoon to butter the bread.

'What do you know about Ben?'

'Nothing, that's the problem. Butter?' he asked, handing her a slice of pre-buttered bread.

'Eh, yes, thank you. Why is it a problem?'

'Because I think he's up to no good. Or rather, I know he's up to no good. Why, what do you think of him?'

'Well,' she said, taking a minute to swallow, 'this is all delicious, by the way. Thank you. Up until the morning we met Sarah, I'd have said he was the perfect gentleman. Since then, he's been giving me a wide berth and I can't work out why.'

'What do you mean?'

'He's suddenly too busy, said he was giving me space, but it's more than that. Maybe he just thinks I'm no longer a link to his mother and therefore can't help him, but you'd think he'd still be grateful for some company while he's here on the island.'

'What, he's saying he doesn't know who his mum is?'

'No, he knows who she is. He just doesn't know anything about her. Says he's doing his family tree and wants to know more about that side of his family.'

'So how did you two get together?'

'Well, firstly, we're not together, as in together. We never have been.' She blushed at the need for clarification. 'But he recognised me instantly. Said his mum's had a photograph of me on her mantelpiece for years.'

Hamish, about to take his next spoonful, paused at her comment. The icy stare he had given Ben the morning they visited Sarah's returned, along with the frown.

'What's wrong?' Anna noticed Hamish physically stiffen at her comment. 'Apparently, she was friends with my mum, and said my photo deserved to be there.' Anna paused. 'What? You don't think that's plausible?'

'I'm not sure. Just be careful. I have a bad feeling about him. What about the other man? The one that was asking about you at the lodge. You'd also seen him, where?'

Filling Hamish in on her visit to Brother's Point, Anna became uneasy again.

'When I thought about it later that night, I managed to rationalise it. He was just a tourist wanting to get back to his car before the light faded completely. But when you mentioned you'd seen him at the lodge, that got me thinking that my initial instincts had been right. I mean, why would he be asking about me?'

'Did you get a good look at him?'

'A little, he was wrapped up for the weather. But I did catch a glimpse of his face.'

'Well, I did.'

'And?'

'I can't quite put my finger on it, but the way he was looking round the outside of the lodge was a bit unnerving. He got jumpy, too, when I appeared.'

'As in, he was acting suspiciously?'

'I thought so.'

'Do you think he and Ben are connected in some way?'

'Sounds a bit far-fetched, but yeah, the thought did cross my mind. His smirk wasn't dissimilar to Ben's either, I thought. And more worryingly, I don't think it's a coincidence that he's on the island at the same time as Ben.'

'I saw him in The Water's Edge, too.'

'Who, the man in black?'

'Yeah, a few nights ago. He and Ben seemed to quietly acknowledge each other. Ben left pretty quickly afterwards, too.'

'You mean they communicated in some way?'

'Yeah, it was just a look, but enough for me to notice. Which reminds me. You said you'd met Ben before, about a year ago?'

Hamish nodded, taking a final mouthful of his soup. 'Do you want a top up?'

'Yes, please.'

'Yeah, he was at the lodge last summer.' He ladled more soup into their bowls. 'It was him, a hundred percent. Wasn't as well-dressed, and he was driving an old banger.'

'That is odd. There's something about his appearance, though, even now, that's off. I just can't put my finger on it.'

'Well, just be careful. If you've made a bit of a connection with the old crow, maybe you don't need his help?'

'Oh, there's no connection, believe me. I'm done with her. But why do you call her that? It's really mean.'

'It's fitting, then,' he said, rising to clear their bowls from the table. 'Can I get you anything else?'

'No, that was delicious. Thank you. Is that the only reason you think Ben's trouble? Because he was here last year? Or is there something else you're not telling me?'

Hamish filled the sink to wash their bowls. He lifted his gaze from the warm water to the view from the window before grabbing their mugs from the coffee table.

Anna found a towel and was poised to dry the dishes; it was the least she could do.

'What is it about him? Please tell me.'

'I honestly don't know, but I'm usually good at spotting trouble. I had to be when I was younger, head things off at the pass, so to speak, before things got out of hand, and I get that feeling with him.'

As Anna watched, the frown that had so often been the driving force in her assumption of him now appeared vulnerable. His eyes, although still moody and piercing, she now understood to be concerned. His stare most definitely shyness.

Leaving him to put the dishes away, she stood by the fire. The roaring flames warmed her to her core. The views out across the North Atlantic had now gone as daylight had given way to darkness, leaving only a sporadic sprinkling of lights, alluding to life in the distance.

'I take it you haven't always lived on the island?'

'No, but I've been here about five years.'

'And have you always lived here, in the cottage?'

'No, I came to help out the old man, stayed with the old crow up the hill for about a year, and then moved in here about four years ago.'

'Are you going to tell me why you call her an *old crow*?'

'That one's maybe for another day. Don't want to go ruining what's turned into a nice evening.'

His comment caused her to remember her earlier bout of sobbing, and how she felt when he'd held her. Which, in turn, caused her to blush. Hamish was obviously aware and was chuckling, which didn't help.

'I'd offer you a glass of wine, but you've to drive later.'

'That's okay. I should really get going, anyway. I have a magazine article to write and the deadline's looming.'

A few seconds of awkward silence followed. His stare, just as intense, had become seductive.

'I'll get your coat.'

As his broad shoulders held her coat open, she slipped her arms through the sleeves. His hands helped her – or was he caressing her? She turned to thank him, only to find she had no trouble interpreting his expression.

His gaze was on her lips; his arms pulled her close. Desire swept through her body as they became lost in a passionate kiss, ridding Anna of any doubts she may have had about the expressionless man with intensely piercing eyes.

CHAPTER TWENTY-TWO

Lying in bed, Hamish struggled to sleep, the events of the evening still preying on his mind. He had kissed Anna, the woman he'd loved since he'd first set eyes on her in The Water's Edge. And she had kissed him back.

But for Hamish, that had made whatever was going on at the lodge all the more worrying. The woman he loved was most probably in danger. And to protect her, he had no option but to be dishonest with her, at least for the time being.

While Anna didn't know the truth about Ben, she couldn't change her behaviour towards him and start acting; that would most definitely alert Ben to the fact he'd been rumbled.

Hamish rolled onto his back, the ceiling offering no clarity. He knew he needed to up his game if he was going to get to the bottom of what was happening with Ben, the other man dressed in black, and the lodge. And he had to do it quickly before Ben achieved whatever goal he was chasing.

And it didn't matter how much Hamish considered the options, he kept coming to the same conclusion. There was only one logical explanation surrounding Ben's reappearance at the lodge, sheet of paper in hand: Ben thought he could lay claim to The Old Lodge. Hamish was under no doubt that this would ignite another fire, meaning he was also going to have to find a resolution between Iain and the old crow.

But no matter the course of action Hamish decided to take, he was going to have to do it quickly and in a way that Anna could forgive him afterwards. She needed to know she could trust him and that whatever he did, whatever he didn't tell her, it was to protect her, Iain, and the lodge.

His first port of call had to be his mum.

CHAPTER TWENTY-THREE

Throughout a morning spent repairing old sheep pens, Hamish's thoughts had never been far from Anna, Ben, and the lodge. And now that he was stopping for lunch at his cottage, he knew it was time to speak to his mum.

He pulled his mobile from his pocket and his thumb scrolled through his contacts before hitting the icon of the woman whose past he was about to drag up. Several rings, not unusual he decided; she was always on the go.

'Hello, son.'

'Hi, mum. How are you?'

'All the better for hearing your voice, love.'

'How's Iain?'

'He's good. He's had a time of it with Sarah. Again,' she emphasised. 'But the break's doing him good. Anyway, how are you?'

Despite going over the conversation several times during the morning, Hamish was struggling to find his words.

'Your silence sounds serious. What's wrong, son? Sarah hasn't found out who you are, has she?'

'No, but that might not be for much longer.'

'Why, what do you mean?' his mum said, her voice wavering.

As he recited the recent events, Hamish tried to play down his concerns around Ben. But his mum was an intelligent woman, and given she was not one to mince her words, she was quick to work out Hamish's concerns for herself.

'Hold on—'

'Go and put the kettle on, Maggie,' Hamish heard Iain say. 'I just want a word with the lad.'

The phone was passed over and Hamish heard Iain clearing his throat.

'Hello, lad. So, out with it. What are you really thinking?'

'I'm thinking this Ben has his sights on The Old Lodge. Please tell me he has no claim to it?'

'No, Susanna was sensible when it came to the lodge. She kept it completely separate to everything else and, because of Sarah, Susanna also kept it in her name, although Sarah doesn't know that.'

'Right, okay, well that piece of information we keep just between us.'

'Anyway, they can't just appear and claim a building they're not entitled to.'

'Agreed, but I'm telling you, there's something about the lodge that's got their interest piqued, I've just no idea what. And there's more, Iain. It's just a coincidence, timing-wise, but Anna has discovered she has links to the lodge and—'

'Anna's there?'

'Yes, well not here, I mean she was, but not now, no. She's living on the island, has been for a few years. I've seen her around, but I didn't realise who she was until a few days ago. You'll know who I mean. It's the girl who's always taking photographs.'

'That's-that's Anna?'

'Yeah, but it gets worse, Iain. This Ben has wheedled his way in.'

'Right, well, she needs protected from whatever he's up to. And it's the same lad as last year, you're sure?'

'Definitely.'

'I need to get back then. The shit may be about to hit the fan and we'll all need to be there for Anna when it does. Try and keep her away from the lodge, if you can, in the meantime. I'll pass you back over to your mum and I'll get back to the island tomorrow.'

'Well, come to mine. There's no point in you being up at the cottage with the old crow, and it's maybe better if Ben doesn't see you anyway.'

'Right, okay. Here's your mum.'

'Hi, son. Let me—'

'There's more, mum. He's told her about the photograph on your mantelpiece.'

'He—what? How does he know about that?'

'I don't know. But what worries me more is he's said he recognised her from it. Which is rubbish – she's about five years old in that photo. I've seen Anna around the island for the last couple of years and never recognised her. So, I reckon he's had to get to know her. He's asked about the girl who's always photographing the lodge and then I'm guessing he got a hell of a shock when he's realised who she is.'

'She photographs the lodge?' his mum said, her voice breaking.

'Yeah, all the time. And purely because she loves it.'

CHAPTER TWENTY-FOUR

Having spent the morning editing the photographs she'd taken at Brother's Point, Anna was in the loft, printing out those she thought had potential as she tried to find a series that would work seamlessly as a collection.

Her evening with Hamish was never far from her thoughts as she rearranged the prints in various orders as the light from the Velux windows brought them to life. Anna eventually found a sequence she was happy with. And just as she was about to make the final edits to her selected images, her phone pinged.

Hey, do you fancy some company tonight?

Yeah. She tried to appear laid-back. *What do you have in mind?*

I could be at yours for seven. I'll bring dinner.

Oh, even better!

Just have your oven on so it can be reheated. You do have an oven??? He joked.

Yes!!!!!!!!!

Phone cast aside, Anna set about tidying her cottage. It was clean, though there were a few discarded fleeces and photography magazines lying around her living room. And photographs for her next magazine article were splayed across her breakfast bar, along with the draft article.

Making sure everything was in its place, she puffed the cushions on the sofa and restocked the logs kept by the wood burner, before doing her dishes.

Next was her bedroom. Having no family and few friends on the island meant she wasn't used to having visitors. Rob and Andy would call in on the odd occasion they had time off, but if anything was wrong, they would be there at a moment's notice.

Smiling to herself, Anna remembered the morning she had woken up to find her kitchen floor drenched in water after her washing machine had leaked. Having first called a friend who was a plumber, Rob and Andy had then appeared within half an hour and helped her clean up, staying until the plumber had fixed the problem before slipping him enough money to ensure Anna wouldn't have to worry about a bill falling through her letterbox.

Or the time she'd had the flu. Rob had arrived, bringing half the local pharmacy with him, along with a selection of ready-to-eat meals from Andy.

Stopping to wonder what on earth she would have done without the two men in her life, Anna picked up her phone.

I won't be down for dinner tonight, but because I don't say it often enough, you two are awesome. Love you both. xx

She brought her attention back to her bedroom. There was every chance the conversation could get around to her photography and, in turn, her converted loft – meaning the array of clothes and bags currently hanging from, or draped across, her spiral staircase needed to be re-homed.

Her thoughts turned to what she should wear. Having turned into a snivelling mess the night before, she was determined to make an impression tonight.

After a quick shower, Anna blow-dried her hair, applied a little make-up, and opted for her favourite jeans, the ones she'd worn the day Hamish had rescued her from the barn. Rifling through her wardrobe, she found a boat-necked dress jumper, not so thick that she would melt by the wood burner, but not so thin that she would freeze when away from it.

She was just setting two places at the breakfast bar when there was a knock at her door. After a quick check of her hair in the mirror, she rushed to answer, excitement fluttering in her stomach.

Hamish, his eyes as intense as always, his expression soft, kissed her gently as he stepped inside.

She took his coat and hung it up while he placed dinner on the breakfast bar.

'You look nice.' His arms pulled her close.

'So do you.' She blushed, their lips meeting in a kiss that caused her body to go limp against his; their arms holding each other close.

He pulled away, but Anna was aware his seductively enticing eyes were still lost in hers.

'I've wanted to kiss you for a long, long time,' he said.

'You have?'

'Yeah, I have.'

Now it was his turn to blush.

'I always thought you didn't like me.'

'I always thought you wouldn't be interested in me.'

She caressed his stubbled cheek before her arms enveloped his neck. His hands caressed her back. They kissed. It was long and passionate, and left Anna in no doubt about their feelings for each other.

He unpacked dinner. 'Andy said we'd to get this in the oven quickly.'

'You went to The Water's Edge?'

'Yeah, and I've had quite the interrogation. So, when you

report back – and you'll have to, believe me – my lips were nowhere near yours.'

'Oh, I'm sorry.' She giggled.

'It's fine. It's good you've had them in your life. Interrogated by two dads, though – that's a first.'

'You mean Andy left the kitchen?'

'Yeah, he delivered dinner into my hands personally, before telling me he could now pick me out of a line-up.'

And as they both fell into fits of laughter, she placed Andy's ovenproof dish into the oven.

'He said give it thirty minutes, stir, and serve.'

'What is it?' She sniffed in an effort to garner a whiff of Andy's delicacy.

'I've no idea, I didn't get to choose. I asked Rob what you liked and never got another word in after that.' He chuckled. 'This one's to go in the fridge,' he said, pulling out a second container.

'What is it?'

'All I know is it's dessert.'

'Oh, wow.' She leaned forward to open the lid. 'His desserts are to die for.'

'Eh, no. Andy said I'd to keep that one as a surprise. And I'm doing as I'm told. There's two of them and they're feisty,' he joked. 'This one's for the fridge as well. Looks like it might be cream,' he said, taking a smaller container from the bag.

TUCKING INTO SPANISH HOTPOT FOLLOWED BY LEMON MERINGUE pie and cream, Anna felt completely at ease in Hamish's company. There were no awkward silences, just laughter and chatter as they spoke about their lives on the island.

Once they'd finished dinner, Hamish worked his way around the prints on her wall while Anna made them coffee.

'They're stunning. I'd no idea you were so good.'

'Gee, thanks,' Anna replied.

'No, I mean, I'd no idea you were such a professional.' He smiled as he sat on the sofa.

'That's better.' She chuckled, handing him a mug and joining him. 'Do you want to watch a movie?' She leaned into him, his arm wrapping around her.

The heat from the wood burner. Hamish holding her close. His lips kissing the top of her head while she sipped her coffee. It was bliss, and as one movie turned into two, Anna knew she didn't want the evening to end.

But a knock on the front door at almost midnight caused them both to jump. 'It'll be Mrs Stewart,' Anna announced. 'I hope her husband's okay. He doesn't keep well.'

As she opened the door, she knew her blissful evening had come to an abrupt end.

'What do you want?' she managed, standing tall and trying to maintain eye contact, as though the man's presence wasn't fazing her at all.

But just as he took a step across the threshold, Hamish appeared at the door. He towered over their intruder by a good foot, putting his broad shoulders between Anna and their unwanted visitor.

'Sorry, wrong house,' the man said, and without a backward glance, the man in black from Brother's Point walked off towards the main road.

While Hamish locked the door behind them, Anna rushed to check the back door was also locked. 'What the hell was he doing here?'

'I don't know, but we need to talk.'

'What's wrong?' She noticed his expression was the same as when he had found Ben in Sarah's cottage.

'I'm not sure. The fact that guy's turned up here, though, isn't good, especially at this time of night. No, they're up to something and I need to find out what.'

He pulled her closer, his arms enveloping her just as they had done the night before.

'You trust me, don't you?'

'Yes,' she said, pulling away. 'Of course. Why?'

'Because I'm going to ask you to pack a bag and go and stay at The Water's Edge for a few days, just until I get to the bottom of what's going on.'

'You mean you think I'm in danger?'

'Why else was that guy at your door? I mean, it's almost midnight.'

'So why do you think he was at Brother's Point?'

Hamish's frown was enough to let Anna know that wasn't a question he wanted to answer.

'What, you mean if there hadn't been a dog walker around—'

'You'd be in the sea, yeah, I think so.'

Feeling sick, Anna began to pace the room. 'No, surely not. There must be another explanation.'

'Anna, believe me.' He caught her on the passing and pulled her to sit beside him. 'You need to believe me when I say there is more to Ben than you realise. I can't protect you when you are way over this side of the island, and I need to know you're safe. I have to be at The Old Lodge. I have to find out what's going on and protect the old man.'

'You mean my grandfather?'

'Well, that's something we'll need to talk about later. In the meantime, go pack a bag.'

'What, you're serious?'

'Very.'

As Anna went to gather her things, Hamish worked around her, ensuring the rest of the cottage was secure.

'We need to take your jeep with us. They can't think you're here. It would only encourage them to break in. We need to make sure we keep their interest over at the lodge.'

Hamish pulled his phone from his pocket.

'Hey, sorry to call you this late. Would it be okay if I left a vehicle parked at yours for a few days? It would need to be somewhere out of sight.' He looked out of the window. 'Of course, it's legit. It belongs to a-a friend of mine. She just needs a place to park it for a few days, that's all.'

Anna placed a small suitcase by the door. His tone seemed to soften.

'Thanks, mate, the back shed, that would be perfect. Yeah, yeah, next few pints are on me.'

Hamish scanned the living room before turning the lights off. 'You ready to go?'

'Yeah, I just need to grab my laptop from upstairs.'

'Upstairs?'

'Yeah, upstairs.' She smiled.

Hamish followed. 'That's some staircase,' he said, crouching his head as his broad shoulders ascended the staircase with some trouble. 'Wow, this is fantastic.'

'Isn't it!' she gushed.

'Anna,' he said, struggling to stand upright as he cast his eyes around the room, 'you're brilliant. Do you sell these? I mean, you must, with this set up? It's fantastic.'

'Well, one day, if you'll let us sit and chat without telling me I've to go into hiding, I could tell you a bit more about myself.'

Dropping on to the stool next to her, Hamish straightened his back and pulled her onto his lap. 'We will. I want to hear everything about you. I also want to be able to kiss you every day, and I'll not be able to do that while you're at The Water's Edge. I'll get chased out by you-know-who and you-know-who.' He smiled. 'So, believe me when I say I'm going to do everything I can to get to the bottom of whatever's going on. Quickly. And I'm going to keep you safe.'

She leaned in and her lips met his. Her fears washed away,

lost in a moment of excitement. But it was all too brief. Tonight couldn't be the night.

Following Hamish outside, she locked her cottage and took the spare key from its hiding place.

'Here's my keys. You take the Land Rover,' he instructed, loading her belongings into the back. I'm going to drive your jeep.'

'Why?'

'Because I'm taking no chances. You follow me, okay. I'm going to turn off just before we go into Portree. There's a croft where we can hide your jeep for a few days. But if a car comes along behind us, I'll keep driving into town. I'm only turning off if there's no one behind us, okay? If we get separated, you drive straight to The Water's Edge – promise.'

The wind swept down from the north. Anna pulled her jacket around her as their words disappeared in a haze of white steam from the chilly air.

'Why don't we just call the police?' Anna leaned in further, in an attempt to be heard against the gusts.

'What has Ben done wrong? What has the guy in black done wrong? It's all speculation just now.'

'Then why are you so scared for me?'

'Because something's not right. I can feel it in my gut, and I'm not taking any chances by leaving you here. So, follow me. We'll drop off your jeep, then I'll take you to Rob and Andy.'

PULLING OUT ONTO THE MAIN ROAD IN A LAND ROVER THAT smelled of collie and sheep, Anna followed Hamish towards Portree. And true to his word, about half a mile from town, he turned off onto a dirt track.

In the pitch dark, and driving a strange vehicle up a road she didn't know, the events of the evening began to sink in. Anna found her imagination getting the better of her. And the more she thought about it, the more she realised she didn't know Hamish either. For all she knew, they could be in it together and she had just been naively lured to whatever-the-hell place this was.

'Shit!'

Should she just stop? But if she stopped, he would stop. Panic rose in her stomach like a torrid wave. Where the hell was she? She grabbed her phone. No signal. Her heart beat overtime; the thudding in her ears deafening, almost painful.

Lights in the distance. Hamish slowed in front of her as they drove across a cattle-grid, alerting her to the fact they had just crossed into another crofter's land. The lights came closer. She looked at his fuel gauge – more than enough to get herself back to Portree. All she had to do was make sure no one got in beside her. She checked her door; the Land Rover was old enough that the doors locked with push-down buttons. She locked her door, and the one behind, then she reached across, her fingertips winning in their battle to secure the passenger side. That just left the rear passenger door, which she knew she would never reach without stopping.

Slowing, Hamish came to a halt. A man came rushing from a farmhouse and ran over to unlock a barn door. Hamish drove in. Anna's heart raced as she watched. Her hands gripped the wheel, ready to about-turn at a moment's notice.

But with Hamish reappearing moments later, and the other man closing and locking the barn doors behind him, Anna was brought momentarily out of her panic. She watched as both men shook hands. Hamish ran towards the Land Rover and threw her a look that meant everything was okay.

Anna unlocked her door before clambering into the passenger seat, allowing Hamish to jump behind the wheel. She threw her arms around his neck.

'You okay?'

'Yeah, my imagination just got the better of me there for a

bit, that's all. It's just, it's turned into a strange night.'

'You can say that again.'

They set off across the cattle grid.

'And not the night I had planned.' He winked, leaning across to give her a kiss.

'Dinner was good, though,' she joked. 'How long do you think I'll need to stay at Rob and Andy's for?'

'Hopefully just a couple of days.'

'Hamish, what are you going to do? I mean, should I be worried?'

'Are you worried about me?'

He was teasing her, but his delight at her concern for him was obvious.

'Of course I'm worried about you, but would you be serious for a minute?'

'I'm not being serious because I don't want you worrying. But, on saying that, you need to promise me you'll stay at The Water's Edge until I come back. You won't leave, not even to wander around Portree. You'll stay put.'

IN THE CAR PARK OUTSIDE THE WATER'S EDGE, HAMISH HELPED Anna retrieve her belongings from the back of the Land Rover.

'Will they still be open?'

'It's okay, I have a key. Home from home, remember.'

'Come on then,' Hamish said, lifting her bags. 'Let's get you safely inside.'

'No, I'll go on my own. I'm not giving them the worry. I'll tell them my jeep's broken down – that'll buy us a few days.'

'You're going to lie to them?'

'Yeah, I'm not bringing this to their door.'

'Are you sure?' he said, pulling her close, his arms reassuringly safe.

'I am.'

CHAPTER TWENTY-FIVE

Having driven non-stop from Aberdeen, Iain arrived at Hamish's cottage early-afternoon. And grateful for the spare key Hamish had insisted he keep, Iain was able to let himself in, light the fire, and make a bite to eat.

Rubbing at his old bones, Iain couldn't help but wonder what the next few days would bring. He had found little peace since Susanna had passed away just over a year ago. The lodge had become unbearably lonely. And although he had taken Sarah in, given her a roof over her head, she'd had little empathy or compassion for his loss, his grief, or his battle to go on in a world without the woman he had loved unconditionally for almost sixty years.

And he couldn't help but feel there was more heartache to come. Anna being on the island was something he would no doubt have to face sooner or later. But the version of the past she knew would make that easier. The last thing he wanted to do was shatter any illusions she had of her mother. He knew deep down he would take the hit. Better she hated him than Helena.

The mere thought of Helena brought tears to his eyes.

Susanna had never been the same after their daughter's death; it had been the start of a steady deterioration in her health. But it had also resulted in them having endless conversations about the past.

They had wanted Helena to be as far away from Sarah as was possible, but not at the detriment of their relationship. But Helena was feisty, her troublesome teens continuing into her twenties. She was moody and Iain knew she disliked him, because she felt he never stood up to Sarah. But he did, in a quiet and effective way, and if Helena had stuck around, she would have discovered there was more to their family's past than she realised. But Helena had wanted to be free, had wanted to paint, and the last thing he wanted to do was stand in her way.

He looked around Hamish's cottage – a far cry from how it had looked when he'd decorated it for Helena and Anna, never thinking at the time that they would never set foot in it.

'Hi, Iain.'

'Hamish, lad. How are you?'

'I'm fine. I spotted the smoke from the chimney and thought I'd check on you. I need to get some kindling, though, so if you're alright here, I'll be about an hour.'

HAMISH PARKED AROUND THE BACK OF THE OLD LODGE. HE got out and retrieved his axe, heading straight for the log pile to get started on the kindling. He found it surprisingly therapeutic, and he was happy to take on the task when stocks were running low. Since the lodge had become vacant around the same time last year, Hamish had been using its ample wood supply to keep him, Sarah and Iain going through the winter months.

Once he'd tossed enough kindling into the back of his Land Rover, Hamish drove up to the cottage at the top of the hill.

He turned off the engine, pausing for a moment to take a

breath before he opened the door. Visiting Sarah was never easy and as he went to gather up an armful of kindling from the back of his Land Rover, he found himself mustering up the energy to tolerate her nonsense. Walking into Sarah's cottage, arms laden, Hamish headed for the kindling bucket and began to top it up.

'About bloody time. I thought I was going to have to chop the feckin stuff myself,' snarled Sarah from her armchair.

'Now, Sarah, you know I'd never let you run out,' Hamish said through gritted teeth.

'Don't give me any of your lip. Just get out there and do what you're paid to do. Bloody useless help.'

'It's not you who pays me, though, is it? So keep your snide comments to yourself, Sarah, and be grateful for what people do for you around here.'

'Feck off, go on, get.'

Hamish got on his feet and headed back to the Land Rover, leaving the old crow to fester. But not before spotting the leather-bound notebook firmly in her grasp and a glistening on her cheeks that he was sure had been caused by tears.

The scene unsettled him. Never in all the years he had known Sarah had he ever seen any hint of emotion or feelings. She had been constant in her coolness, quick to snarl and as bitter as winds that howled down from the north.

On his descent towards The Old Lodge, Hamish stopped to check the outbuildings. The first two were locked, as usual, and the third still had its dodgy padlock. Hamish cursed himself for forgetting to buy a new one.

BACK AT THE COTTAGE, IAIN HAD BEGUN PREPARING DINNER. 'Least I could do, lad. Anyway, it's better than doing nothing.'

'Well, all's calm at the lodge, and I doubt anyone will appear now. It's far too dark.'

'So, what exactly do you think's going on?'

'I don't know. I mean, we have Anna, who genuinely loves the lodge. She's only become involved because she happened to be there photographing it each time Ben was there.' Hamish paused to take a sip of the coffee Iain had made him. 'Then we have Ben, who has done nothing wrong, other than to say he is Mum's son.' He looked at Iain. 'Maybe that is a crime. We could say that's impersonation. Do you reckon he's using that name so he's more likely to be left to look around in peace?'

Iain scratched his chin but said nothing.

Hamish continued. 'That takes us to how does he know the name and why is he looking around? Why is he so interested in the lodge, and why does he always have that crumpled piece of paper stuck to his hands?'

'I haven't told you, lad, but I've had several offers since Susanna passed, and to be honest, I left him to look around because I presumed he was just another interested party who would come along with an offer. Not,' he emphasised, 'that I'm thinking of selling. It's just that I honestly don't know what to do.' He shook his head. 'The Old Lodge has been such a big part of my life, and for so long. It was always full. There were always people in our lives, and now the world's gone silent, lad. It's just stopped turning for me.' He rubbed his face in his hands and seemed to be looking anywhere but at Hamish. 'He had a key, and I guess grief meant I didn't care enough. I didn't ask for his name, I just let him look around.'

'Didn't you wonder how he had a key?'

'Aye, aye, I did, but as I said, grief just makes you not give a damn. The lodge means nothing without Susanna in it.'

'Iain, you lost Susanna and you moved out of the lodge. There's no one more sympathetic to that than me, you know that. But we need to get to the bottom of what's going on. There's been another man at the lodge, only once, but he was watching Anna. We need to be worried about him, Iain. He was watching Anna at Brother's Point, gave her a scare.'

'What? Do you think they're connected in some way?'

'They could easily be related. There's a similarity between them. In their age, too. And I think it's too much of a coincidence that they're both sniffing around the lodge and both showing an interest in Anna. The other one turned up at her door about midnight last night.'

'What, Anna's door?' Iain's shock and concern evident.

Hamish nodded.

'Is she okay?'

'Yeah, she's fine. I was with her.'

'You-you were at her cottage?' Iain said, looking confused. 'Anna's cottage?'

'Eh, yeah,' Hamish replied, setting two places at the table.

'At midnight?'

'Yeah.'

'Oh, you were, were you?'

Hamish waited for him to get to his point.

'Well, lad, I think we'd better get to the bottom of it all, then, and quickly.'

'And there's something else,' Hamish added, 'it might be nothing, but Sarah's acting strange.'

'Strange? In what way.'

'Well,' Hamish went on, 'I've noticed her clutching an old leather-bound notebook recently. She was holding it again today, and I'm sure she'd been crying.'

'Ah, okay.' Iain appeared concerned. 'Thanks, lad, I'll check on her.'

'What, you know what's going on, with the notebook, I mean?'

'Aye, I'm afraid so. I need to talk to her first, though. But before I do'—he stiffened, as though bracing himself for the answer—'you're absolutely sure that this Ben and the other fella look alike?'

'Yeah, I'm sure.'

CHAPTER TWENTY-SIX

Sarah was warming her frail hands by the Aga when Iain appeared at the back door of the cottage.

'Evening, Sarah.'

'I wasn't expecting you back until later in the week.'

'Yeah, well, I'd to cut the trip short. We, eh, we need to talk, Sarah.' He noticed the leather-bound notebook on the table.

'I know.' Her cheeks damp with tears, she turned to face him. 'I'd know him anywhere, Iain.' Tears flooding her cheeks, she wiped them away with a tissue.

'They're both here.'

Sarah let out a gasp. Iain rushed forward to steady her as her frail limbs fell into a chair. She supported herself with the table. 'You've seen them, both of them?'

'No, but Hamish has.'

'Hamish knows?' she barked.

'No, he hasn't a clue, he just thinks it's two opportunists up to no good.'

'Hmm.' She shrugged. 'Well, he'd be right, wouldn't he.'

'But I warned you last year, when that *Ben*,' he said rolling his eyes, 'first turned up. There has to be a reason that he's here again.'

'I know. But I don't understand why he's calling himself Ben. And he was with Anna. What the hell are the two of them doing together? He, he's roped her in, hasn't he?' She sobbed.

'No, no he hasn't. But I'm convinced he's using her to get to something. And I'll be honest, Sarah. I'm worried about her. I-eh, I'm sorry to say it, but she's not safe around them.'

Sarah was shaking uncontrollably. Iain knew life had taunted her. It had given her everything only to rip it all away. Tearing her world apart. Robbing her of those most precious to her and abandoning her to a life she couldn't allow herself to live. She existed day to day, waiting for the day when she would finally be free. Free of heartache. Free of the feeling of eternal loss. And free of pain.

Iain finished making tea and placed two mugs on the table. Noticing her wince as her frail hands clasped her mug, Iain took her medication from the cupboard.

'You haven't taken any tablets since I left. You can't keep doing that, Sarah, or you'll never get rid of me. I won't be able to leave you.' He tried to lighten the mood, given he was telling her off, again. 'Don't have me wasting my time putting them into those weekly trays for you. You just need to tip them out into your palm.'

Sarah's silence was deafening.

'Sarah, please,' he begged, placing her tablets in front of her with a glass of water. 'Why do you keep doing this to yourself?'

'Because I was allowed to live,' she managed.

Iain hung his head. Over the years, he had watched as his sister withdrew into herself. The lively young woman he had known, with a mischievous sense of humour and a zest for life, had disappeared, leaving in her place an empty, cold soul.

Susanna and Iain had tried everything over the years, but he had realised long ago that he couldn't help his sister if she didn't want to be helped. Her grief was too deep. All he could do was make sure she lived the remainder of her life in as much comfort as she would allow. And make sure she had everything she needed, no matter the verbal abuse that would come his way.

Iain had always known her bitter retorts were never aimed at him or anyone else for that matter who happened to be on the receiving end of her sharp tongue. He knew not to take it personally. It appeared Sarah was fighting her own internal battle. One she had lost through her own guilt.

He could see it consumed her every waking minute. Not taking her medication seemed like a way of punishing herself. Physical pain to stave off the emotional pain.

'I have a feeling there's going to be trouble, Sarah. And we need to be prepared for it.' He went on to tell her about the other man and how he had appeared at Anna's door.

'She looks nothing like her, you know.'

'Who?'

'Anna, she looks nothing like Helena.'

'So I've heard.' Iain sighed, worrying at the thought of the reaction he might get when he did finally meet Anna.

'You need to brace yourself,' Sarah managed, stopping to sip her tea.

'Me, why?'

'She's a young Susannah, but with my eyes. She has my eye colour.'

Iain sat in silence, his own turbulent emotions taking hold until Sarah dragged him from his thoughts.

'Well, do you have a plan?' Sarah's hand reached for the notebook. 'Or is there something else you need to tell me?'

Iain rubbed his face in his hands. 'We need to get to the bottom of why they are here. And'—he glanced at Sarah—'we need to know why he is calling himself Ben.'

'He's probably just plucked a name out of thin air,' quipped Sarah.

'I don't think he has. He knows about a photo of Anna, taken when she was only five or six years old.'

A frown spread across Sarah's forehead as she tried to join the dots. 'So, he's been to Aberdeen?'

'Yes.'

'How do you know?'

A sigh escaped Iain's lips. 'Do you remember the middle names of all those who lived in Aberdeen.'

'Middle names?' Sarah was confused.

Iain raised his eyebrows, encouraging her to think a little deeper.

Sarah's hands cupped her face. 'What? You mean—'

'Yes. I'm sorry I didn't tell you. It just felt easier, and kinder, given the past.'

'All this time.' Sarah's eyes teared again. 'He's been here, all this time?'

CHAPTER TWENTY-SEVEN

Anna was spending the evening helping Rob and Andy. Something she would occasionally do if they were short staffed. But tonight, quite simply, she needed to keep her mind occupied. High-vis Jim was in his usual spot at the bar, and even with the lateness in the year, there was still an even mix of tourists and locals.

'Tray for table four, Susie.'

After delivering the drinks order, Anna began pushing chairs in and tidying up. She checked in with customers that everything was okay as she passed.

Battling her way through the bustling restaurant with another order, Anna spotted a lady sitting in the corner looking utterly uncomfortable. The lady – mid-fifties, Anna guessed – appeared to have tucked herself so far into the corner, it was as if she didn't want to be there.

'Everything okay?' Anna asked on passing.

'Eh, yes, thank you.'

'Are you ready to order or would you like a few minutes?'

'I'm actually waiting on a friend.'

'No problem. Would you like to order a drink while you wait?'

'A white wine, please. Pinot, if you have it.'

'Certainly.'

Anna was just about to walk away when the lady stopped her with a question.

'Are you local?'

About to come out with her usual spiel about her mother being from the island, Anna paused, instead replying, 'Yes.' She smiled. 'Are you on holiday?'

'Something like that.'

'I'll get your wine,' Anna said, 'and I'll come back and take your order once your friend's arrived.'

Intrigued by both the woman's tone and response, Anna returned to the bar. Rob gave her one of his I'm-so-happy-you're-here smiles as she picked up the next drinks order. And as she continued to deliver drinks and clear tables, Hamish was never far from her thoughts. She'd texted him, but he hadn't replied. At the best of times the signal could be ropey at the lodge, so she tried not to worry.

Passing the bar, Anna picked up a glass of Pinot and headed towards the lady in the corner. Her friend was just arriving, taking her coat off and settling into her chair. And just as she approached, Anna realised who it was. 'Crissie.'

'Anna.'

Crissie appeared both delighted and flustered to see her.

'Oh, if I'd known you were meeting Crissie, I'd have snuck you a large,' Anna joked. But the lady in the corner now appeared more flustered and uncomfortable than ever.

'Oh, yes, this-this is my friend. We're just having a catch up. I'll have the same, thank you,' Crissie said, nodding to the glass of Pinot.

When Anna returned to the bar, Rob had caught up with

orders and was wiping the bar top and taking stock of the emptying shelves.

'We've kept you on your toes tonight.' He laughed.

'You sure have,' said High-vis Jim, joining in from the corner.

'I wouldn't have it any other way.' Anna picked up the second glass of Pinot.

She placed it in front of Crissie and asked, 'Are you ladies ready to order, or would you like another minute?'

Her request was met with silence as the two ladies looked at each other awkwardly.

'I can come back, if you'd like a little longer?'

'It's okay, love,' Crissie's friend replied. 'I think we're both going for the fish on the specials board.'

'No problem. It won't be too long.' Anna smiled, turning to leave.

'Anna, is everything alright?'

Crissie caught her arm.

'Yes, why?'

'Are you working here?'

'Unofficially, I'm staying with Rob and Andy for a couple of days, so I'm mucking in. It's better than sitting upstairs all night on my own. Anyway, I don't mind it.'

'Why are you staying? If you don't mind me asking.'

'Oh, eh, I'm just-just spending a couple of days with them, that's all.'

THE EVENING SLIPPED BY, AND AS THE MEAL ORDERS SLOWED, Anna was able to take a breath and slow down long enough to venture across to Crissie and her friend, who she had noticed had been deep in conversation since the moment Crissie had arrived.

Stopping to let a customer pass by, Anna inadvertently over-heard their conversation.

'So why are you really here, Maggie? I mean, after all these years?'

'I'm here to see Iain at The Old Lodge.'

'Gosh, it's been a lot of years since you were last over there.'

'It'll be strange'—she nodded—'being back there, especially without Susanna. You know how it was, he and Susanna were like parents to me. Iain still is, he's the father I never had. The father Helena should have had.'

'Why do I get the impression there's more to this, Maggie? I mean, it's usually Iain making the trip to see you. Has it got something to do with Anna and Ben?'

'You've seen Ben?'

'Yes, he was in the archive centre. He's been looking into things with Anna.'

'Crissie, that wasn't Ben.'

While Anna tried to make sense of Maggie's final comment, her thoughts turned to Hamish and the grandfather she had come to loathe. But if she had overheard Maggie correctly, neither man knew who they were dealing with. If Ben wasn't who he said he was, then who the hell was he and what else was he capable of? And what about the man in black?

She ran to the kitchen. 'Andy, it's quietened down out there. Can I finish for the night?'

'Sure.'

'Can I borrow your car?'

'You know where the keys are, love. Wait—'

'Thank you.'

With that, Anna was out the door.

CHAPTER TWENTY-EIGHT

Turning onto the track leading up to The Old Lodge, Anna dodged the potholes as best she could. Andy's saloon car was low, meaning she couldn't just speed up the track the way she normally would in her own indestructible jeep.

She approached the final corner; the lodge was in darkness. Hamish would be at his cottage. Anna didn't dare to do a three-point turn on the grass verge, not after all the rain they'd had recently, so she kept going towards the lodge.

Heading onto the remains of the gravel driveway, Anna began turning, only to see torchlight flickering in the sitting room. Could it be Iain? Was he back? There was no car. Maybe he didn't want to alert attention to the fact he was there. A thief would surely have a vehicle, she surmised.

Her headlights now shone directly into the room. Two figures looked out, their torches on her, momentarily blinding her view. The man in black and Ben stood side by side, before running from the room.

The front door of the lodge was closed. Locked, she hoped. If they'd used the back door, she still had time to turn around and get away. In the momentary panic, she forgot she wasn't in her jeep and jerked the car into reverse as she began her three-point turn. But her wheels caught the grass verge and, as she put her foot on the accelerator, they began to spin. The more she accelerated, the more the tyres sank into the wet grass.

Her foot was to the floor, the tyres still spinning. She didn't have long. She leaped from the car and ran as fast as she could towards the track. But knowing they would drive down towards the main road in their bid to find her, she ran up the hill towards the outbuildings and the track behind them that she thought might lead to Hamish's cottage or at least back to the main road.

Her heart beat as she put all her energy into running over the uneven ground. She could hear an engine. Voices shouting from the rear of the lodge. They would see her in their head-lights. She left the track and crawled across the uneven ground, scrambling up the incline she hoped would eventually bring her to the outbuildings.

The engine roaring, she lost her footing, slipping back the way she had come. She dug her fingers into the ground and clawed her way back up. Her arms took her weight as her feet slipped. Headlights shone. She tucked her head into her chest, her body splayed out on the hillside as she tried to hold her footing.

The vehicle about-turned and the lights faded. She had got away with it. Beginning her ascent again, she plunged her fingers in the damp, cold earth. Pulling herself up, she reached the next zig of the track. Torches below her snaked across the landscape. They were nowhere near her. She kept on running. But sheep lying across her path darted, bleating, into the dark-ness, their commotion alerting her assailants to her whereabouts.

'There, she's up there.'

The words echoed across the hillside.

Anna put every ounce of energy she had into running towards the track.

A pothole sent her stumbling. She caught her ankle and her trainer slipped from her foot, along with her trainer sock. She dug deep.

Eventually reaching the outbuildings, Anna headed towards the track behind. But headlights approached, threatening to give away her whereabouts.

She darted towards the last outbuilding in the desperate hope the padlock would still be hanging loose. It was. She grappled with the lock before sliding the door just enough to slip inside, pulling it closed behind her. She fumbled her way in the darkness. Her memories of the barn were vague, and she felt her way around the sheep pens, hoping to find the bale of straw she had huddled into previously.

She heard voices outside. Ben and the man in black were arguing.

'Dylan, no. We need her. She might know where the painting is.'

Startled, Anna thought about the painting she had found alongside her mother's wooden box, safely hidden in her Edinburgh flat.

Did Ben mean that painting? Was it what he'd been after all along? Had everything he'd told her been a lie? To get to her? To get to her mother's painting?

She checked her phone. No signal.

'Dylan, no.'

What the hell was going on out there? Were they back in their car? If they were, surely they would keep driving along the track. They were bound to see it with their headlights.

But the sound of their engine revving and disappearing down the hill unnerved her. Had they just decided to leave? Who was *Dylan*? And, what and how was he connected to Ben?

Anna took a moment to calm her breathing. An acrid smell began filling her nostrils. Smoke? Her head was spinning.

An orange glow now spread towards her from the doorway.

Seconds passed.

She realised what they'd done.

The orange glow now illuminated the barn enough for her to see. There had to be another way out. The heat built. Smoke caught in her throat. The galvanised steel of the sheep pens scalded her hands and legs as she fought her way towards the back of the barn.

The hay bales, now fully alight, sent sparks flying towards her. Frantically, she hit the embers as they landed on her clothing. And with her eyes stinging and her lungs struggling for oxygen, she searched in vain for something that might break through the wooden exterior walls.

CHAPTER TWENTY-NINE

'Just make yourself comfortable, Iain. I'll go and get more logs.'

As soon as Hamish opened the door, the smell of burning filled his nostrils. Momentarily wondering if his chimney had caught alight, he stood back for a better look. But all was fine. As he scanned the countryside, his search for the source of the burning was hampered by the darkness.

He ran around the back of the cottage. The orange glow in the distance alerted him to the fact that its source was well alight.

'Iain. We've got to go. Now!'

'What?' Iain said, making his way out of the cottage. 'Oh hell, no. Is that the lodge?'

'I don't think so,' Hamish said, jumping into his old Land Rover. 'It's too high. The outbuildings maybe.'

Iain followed and tried his mobile, gesturing to Hamish that there was no signal. 'Do you think Sarah can see it from the cottage. She might have used the landline?'

'I hope so. How could she miss it?'

'Any hogs in there just now?' Iain panicked.

'No, not yet.' Hamish threw his Land Rover into the next corner as it sped up the hill.

The thick orange glow spread across the landscape. By the time they reached the outbuildings, the second barn was well alight, as was the roof of the third.

Hamish pulled the Land Rover in at a safe distance from the burning buildings. He got out and ran towards the barns, noticing a hint of petrol in the air.

'Do you smell that?' he shouted back at Iain.

'You haven't been keeping fuel in there, have you?'

'No, no, it's all at the top of the hill.'

Standing back, they watched. Helpless and small against the towering flames.

'It's been arson.'

Iain put his head in his hands. 'I think you're right.'

Hamish kicked the ground beneath him, spinning around as he did. Something caught his eye. Anna's trainer, reflecting the burning, orange glow.

Hamish screamed her name and ran towards the barn.

A moment's indecision as Hamish grappled with the idea of finding a way into the barn allowed Iain to catch up with him. He pulled Hamish back. 'What are you doing?'

Hamish fought to break free. The roof caved in. Flames leaped into the air and embers showered down on them.

Hamish fell to his knees, his shrill scream echoing across the hillside.

Sirens in the distance. The heat of the orange glow penetrated Hamish to his very core. His world shattered. His heart breaking.

They were surrounded by fire engines and high-vis firefighters, running, shouting orders, taking control. Water shot from hoses. Hands grabbed Hamish by the shoulders, pulling him back. Sitting him beside Iain.

Iain was hunched over, fragile and tiny. He wept silent tears. Hamish leaned into him – shattered, broken, inconsolable. The woman he had loved for two long years, the woman who had begun to care for him, was gone. And it was all his fault. He was the one who hadn't replaced the broken padlock.

CHAPTER THIRTY

Anna held on to the arthritic hand. Her lungs coughed out smoke; her eyes burned. She followed her great-aunt's lead through the darkness. Crouching, Anna noticed the smell of damp penetrating the smoke.

Sarah's hand had a vice-like grip. She guided Anna, who was unable to stand upright in the cramped space. Anna limped through the darkness, her ankle swollen and sore, her foot burnt, torn and bloody.

'Not far now.'

Anna, silent, trudged on.

The glow from Sarah's torch finally reflected something shiny in the distance. An opening. Anna felt herself speed up as Sarah led her out into the open hillside. A car, the sound of a collie pining from within.

'Get in. We need to get you down there. They'll be thinking you're a gonner.'

Slumping into the seat, Anna watched as her great-aunt skilfully guided the vehicle cross-country. Sarah drove them onto the zigzagging path, her frail foot keeping up speed.

'Thank you,' Anna managed, her chest resisting her words as she fell into another fit of coughing.

As Sarah guided the vehicle through the darkness, the orange glow that had illuminated the sky had been dampened. The dying embers sent plumes of smoke into the night sky. Headlights illuminated the chaos. Two barns burned to the ground, the other teetering on fragile timbers, firefighters in high-vis running back and forth. An ambulance with its door open. Iain and Hamish sitting by its side.

Sarah's bony hands hitting the horn alerted everyone to her arrival.

WHY WOULD SARAH BRING HERSELF INTO THE CHAOS? IAIN wondered. She pulled in near Hamish, but he was oblivious. High-vis figures ran towards the car, towards Sarah's door.

She wound down her window and shouted. 'Wrong side! Hamish, other side!' Her frail voice fighting through the commotion.

Confused, disorientated, devastated, Hamish lifted his head.

'Passenger side, lad,' Iain said, getting to his feet.

Hamish followed on. Through the chaos of the lights, Iain saw his granddaughter. Her head was back against the car seat. Paramedics strapped an oxygen mask to her face.

'The whisky trail,' Iain managed. 'Sarah's only gone and got her out through the old whisky trail.'

CHAPTER THIRTY-ONE

The following morning, with her foot bandaged, ankle strapped, and various burns, cuts and abrasions treated and dressed, Anna had been allowed home. Rob fussed over her, the epitome of the heartbroken father who had almost lost his daughter.

Andy, always the calm one in times of chaos, was in her kitchen. He had stocked her fridge and was making sure she had enough meals to see her through the rest of the week.

'Are you sure you won't come and stay with us, love?' Andy asked for the hundredth time as he brought her another cup of tea.

'I'm sure. I'd be bored upstairs on my own, unable to do anything. Anyway, I've caused you enough trouble. And at least everything I need is on the ground floor here.'

'As long as you're sure.'

'I am. But, Andy, I'm sorry about your car.'

'The car's fine, love. It just needs a tow out of the mud. We'll go and collect it once the police give us the go-ahead.' He crouched down to give her another hug. 'Right, Rob, come on. Let's go.'

'What? How can we go? Look at her, what she's been through.'

'For goodness' sake, Rob, Hamish is here. Let's give them some space. We'll go and get the restaurant opened. I'm sure Hamish can make her lunch and bring her cups of tea.'

Hamish, trying not to laugh, assured Rob that he would take good care of Anna and call them immediately if they were needed. But Rob insisted on going around in a final flurry of organising and making sure everything was shipshape before Andy eventually dragged him out.

Hamish locked the door behind them. He put more logs in the wood burner before kneeling beside Anna, who was lying on the sofa with her ankle elevated. His fingers caressed her face. Anna couldn't fail to see his sheer relief at her being alive.

'You've had a hell of a shock,' she said, taking his hand in hers.

'I'm the least of my worries.' He smiled. 'Let's just focus on getting you up and running again.' He kissed her gently on the forehead.

'I know you're intentionally not mentioning the elephant in the room, but they'll catch them, don't worry. The police won't let them get far.'

'Hmm,' was all Hamish could manage.

Anna looked down at her foot. After being give a bath at the hospital to help loosen the gravel and mud, she'd been bandaged up with an assortment of stitches, paper stitches, and dressings. Other nasty abrasions and burns had been dealt with, as she'd been cut, torn, and grazed in multiple locations, and her sprained ankle, which had ballooned with an assortment of red, blue, and purple bruising, had been strapped.

She was grateful for the fast-acting painkillers that had been injected into her during the ambulance ride from The Old Lodge to the hospital in Broadford, and she was relieved

Hamish was now ensuring she kept on top of her pain with the medication she'd got when she was discharged.

And as she adjusted her aching body to get comfortable, she knew she looked a state. But none of that mattered. She was grateful for the care she'd received. At least her nails were clean. Deep down, she knew she would be okay. Although, despite the bath working wonders at removing the mud and filth, it had done nothing for the smell of smoke that still lingered in her nostrils.

'There's something I need to tell you, Anna.'

Hamish's face was serious.

'What's wrong?'

'Look, I'm not who you think—'

A rattle on the door caused them both to jump. Hamish looked out of the window. 'It's okay. It's Iain and-and the old crow.' He went to the door to let them in. 'Geez, I'm gonna have to stop calling her that,' he muttered.

'Yes, you are.' Anna chuckled. 'She's gone from zero to hero, that one.'

HAMISH OPENED THE DOOR AND WAITED AS IAIN HELPED SARAH clamber out of his 4x4, but was surprised to see the rear passenger door opening.

'Wow, a full house,' Hamish said, running out to give his mum a hug.

'Hello, son.'

'What a surprise. When did you get here?'

'Last night. I was going to surprise you today, but, well, things have happened.'

'Don't be daft. This is still a great surprise,' he said, giving his mum another hug before turning to Sarah. 'How are you today, Sarah?'

'Nothing's wrong with me. Now let's get inside and see the lass.'

Iain raised an eyebrow towards Hamish. 'But she hasn't said *feck* once this morning. These are strange times, lad.'

Stifling a chuckle, Hamish led them inside.

Sarah had made a beeline for Anna, but Hamish managed to cajole her into taking the armchair by the fire.

Anna was feeling nervous, awkward, and slightly terrified at the presence of her grandfather, but she kept reminding herself that things didn't appear quite as cut and dry as she had thought. She knew she should at least hear him out at a more appropriate time.

She turned to rest her foot on the coffee table, allowing Iain and Maggie a seat on the sofa. Hamish rushed to help, placing cushions under her foot and behind her back, before going to put the kettle on.

Anna wasn't sure why Maggie had accompanied them, but she gave her a polite smile. 'Hello. It's nice to see you again. Please, have a seat.' She pointed to the opposite end of the sofa.

Iain had already taken the seat beside her. Anna could tell by his uncomfortable demeanour that he had no idea what kind of reception his appearance would receive. After the evening they had been through, she couldn't help but feel sorry for him.

'Right, everyone,' Hamish said, breaking the ice. 'I've made tea.' He handed everyone a cup. 'And there's lemon drizzle cake, thanks to Andy.'

After a few minutes of pleasant chit-chat while everyone asked Anna how she was feeling and the prognosis on her foot, ankle and other various abrasions, Anna thanked Sarah again.

'We used to sneak into the old whisky trail when we were young. We always got into trouble, but we didn't care, did we, Iain?' An unusually pleasant smile crossed her face.

'No-no, we didn't.'

'But, Sarah, how did you know I was in the barn?'

'That ruddy dog of yours,' she said, nodding towards Hamish. 'What a bloody commotion. Not shutting up, no matter how many times I told him. When he persisted, I thought I'd better have a proper look. I can't see the lodge from the cottage, but I could see lights on the track between the lodge and the outbuildings. At first, I thought it was you, Iain, coming back from'—her frail fingers pointed towards Maggie—'from Aberdeen, but then the lights stopped, and I could see torches looking all around. It was obvious there was a commotion going on.

'So, I got the ruddy dog in the car, figured I'd just let him loose and he'd send the buggers scampering. I just thought it'd be kids up to no good. I took the back track that comes out behind the outbuildings, but then when I got there, I heard the two men looking for Anna. The only place she could have gone was into that barn with the broken padlock.'

Hamish put his face in his hands.

'Don't be like that. It turned out to be her saving. What if she'd carried on along that track and they'd got hold of her there? No, no. She did the right thing in the end. I backed up to the end of the whisky trail. Been years since I've been in there.' She smirked. 'Decades, anyway. I was about halfway along it when I smelled the smoke. I knew what they'd done.

'But I couldn't get the old hatch to open. I was banging and banging on it,' she said, instinctively rubbing her frail, bruised hand. 'I was calling on Anna, shouting as loud as I could,' Sarah said, becoming distressed.

'It's okay.' Hamish got up and sat on the arm of her chair. 'It's okay. You did a great thing.'

'Well, I-I banged, I shouted, and—' Her tear-filled eyes looked at Anna.

Anna took over. 'I was trying to find a way out. The glow of the fire meant I could see, but the heat was unbearably intense. The hay bales had caught light, and the fire just whipped through them. I'd already stood on something sharp. I'd a searing pain in my foot. But I was scrambling around at the back, trying to see if there was an old door or something, when I felt Sarah's knocking under my feet. I thought it was just something moving at first, but it was the repetitive rhythm. I looked down and there it was, a hatch in the floor. There was a groove and I managed to loosen it enough that it moved. And when I pulled it up, there was Sarah. I couldn't believe it.'

Iain, Maggie, and Hamish hung on their every word.

'Aye, then I told her to shut the ruddy hatch behind her, didn't want the flames following us.'

There was laughter as a hint of the old Sarah returned.

'And the rest is history,' Anna finished.

'It's not quite over yet,' Hamish interjected, intentionally keeping his gaze from Sarah. 'They, eh, they're still at large, and we've no idea where they are.'

'Well, if it helps, Ben isn't the real Ben,' Anna volunteered, looking at Maggie.

'You-you overheard me in the restaurant?' Maggie asked.

Anna nodded.

'Well, maybe this is where we come in, Sarah,' Iain questioned. 'We can't keep harbouring the secrets of the past.'

'Does this have something to do with the notebook?' Hamish asked, looking at Iain.

'Yes, yes it does, lad. Do you want to take it from here, Sarah. Or will I?'

As tears brimmed in Sarah's eyes, she gestured to Iain to take the lead.

'Sarah was married, to a chap called Callum, a right nice chap. They eh'—Iain nodded to Hamish, who was still seated on the arm of Sarah's chair, to put a comforting arm around her—'they were married less than twenty-four hours when

Callum had a heart attack. He was out tending his sheep at the time. We'll never know if anything could have been done to save him as a good while passed between him collapsing and us realising something was wrong. By the time we found him, it was too late.'

Sarah held her face in her hands. Maggie passed her tissues, all the time keeping a comforting hand on her knee. Meanwhile, both Anna and Hamish seemed to get the feeling there was worse to come.

'A few weeks later,' Iain continued, 'Sarah found out she was pregnant. Callum Junior was born in the lodge, a few weeks early, but safely. Susanna had to step in and she helped Sarah deliver him. He was born a good hour before the doctor made it out to us.'

He had his eyes firmly on Sarah. 'He was a braw lad. He loved the croft just as much as I do, and his grandpa before me. He grew up helping out after school and at weekends and then worked with us when he left school.'

Anna could tell this was as much news to Hamish as it was to her.

'What happened?' Hamish pushed gently.

He took a deep breath. 'He married a lass from Portree. Her name was Elsa. They lived in the cottage, at the top of the hill. At that time Sarah was living in the lodge with Susanna and I.' Iain fell silent, visibly upset at what he was about to say.

Hamish gently stroked Sarah's back, comforting her as she sobbed into a tissue. Her frail hand gestured to Iain to continue. 'Keep going.' She sobbed. 'They need to know the truth.'

Taking a breath, Iain continued. 'Callum and Elsa had twin boys. One winter, Sarah was babysitting, well we all were. The boys were staying with us at the lodge. They loved it there, loved the hustle and bustle of the place and we loved having them. They were just three years old. Their mum and dad went across to Portree for dinner. To have an evening to themselves. They were on their way home when—'

As he continued, Iain struggled to watch his sister. 'A car going too fast lost control as it came round a corner towards Callum and Elsa. They didn't stand a chance.'

Aside from Sarah's sobs, silence fell across the room.

After a few moments, Sarah lifted her head. 'The boys stayed with us for a few weeks,' she struggled, 'but I-I just couldn't. I had already lost my husband, now my son and his wife. I couldn't look at the boys. They were the spit of their father. They reminded me every day of all I had lost.'

Reaching into her handbag, she pulled out the leather-bound notebook. Her frail fingers opened the pages slowly to retrieve an assortment of photographs, birth and death certificates, and mementos from another lifetime.

'Susanna and I offered to let the boys stay with us, even offered to do it legally, adopt them, but Sarah, she—'

'She wouldn't have it,' Sarah interrupted. 'I refused, point blank. A decision I have regretted to this day. But a decision I made, nonetheless. The boys were put into foster care, on the mainland.' Sarah's watery eyes turned to Maggie.

An eternity seemed to pass before Maggie gasped, 'No, not Sean and Dylan?'

'Mum, are they—?' Hamish broke off.

'Yes, but I don't understand. How did they end up with me?'

'When the boys went into care,' Iain continued, 'something I have to say Susanna and I struggled with for years, we requested they be placed with you Maggie, but anonymously. Susanna and I knew that if they were with you, they would be safe.'

'But they didn't stay with us for long, Mum?' Hamish questioned.

'No.' Maggie's eyes filled up. 'They were eight when I

slipped and broke my leg. It was a bad break, I'd to get it pinned and was off my feet for a good long while. The boys were taken away. I was seen as unfit to foster during that time, and by the time my leg had heeled and I was fit again, the boys were settled somewhere else and those in charge decided to leave them be. I then had another two children placed with me. But,' she said, realising, 'that's how that Ben will have known about Anna's photo on the mantlepiece. And I inadvertently kept the lodge alive in their minds as I used to tell them bedtime stories, mostly made up, of course, but of life on the croft and at The Old Lodge. They wouldn't have known it was the same place, but it must have resonated with them.'

With everyone deep in thought, silence filled the room. Until Anna, mustered up the courage to ask her all-important question. Turning to Maggie, 'That means that either Sean or Dylan was pretending to be your son?'

Glancing at Hamish, 'Yes.'

Anna caught a fleeting look between Maggie and Hamish. '*Mum?*'

'That's what I was trying to tell you just before-just before everyone arrived. Maggie is my mum, and I came to the island to work for Iain.'

'Keep an eye on how I was treating him, you mean?' Sarah's eyes teared again.

Hamish continued. 'I was pretty sure Ben wasn't who he said he was, but there's more than one Ben Sutherland in the world so I was just going on instinct. I mean, it could have been a coincidence, and I could have been wrong. But I just got that feeling from him, you know, that he was up to no good. But when you mentioned he had said his mother was Maggie Sutherland from Aberdeen, that was when I knew for sure. But if I'd said something, your attitude towards him would have changed. I needed to find out what he was up to and why he was making out he was Ben Sutherland. If you had changed in any way towards him, he might have been scared off.'

'And wouldn't that have been a good thing?' Anna frowned, questioning his motive.

'No, no it wouldn't. I needed to get to the bottom of who he was and why he was impersonating Ben Sutherland.'

'Why?'

'Because, I'm Ben Sutherland.'

'What?' Anna exclaimed.

'I'm Ben Sutherland.'

Hamish looked at his mum; she gave him a reassuring smile.

'And you knew, Iain? You knew all this time that he was Maggie's son?' Sarah asked, her tone as fragile as her arthritic fingers.

'Aye, aye I did.'

'So, who's Hamish?' Anna asked, struggling to keep a scolding tone out of her voice.

'I'm Hamish. Hamish is my middle name. Ben was my dad's name and I've always gone by Hamish.'

'He has. I've called him Hamish since he was a toddler, since his dad left,' Maggie interjected.

'But you said your surname was McPherson?'

'It is. My dad's Ben McPherson.'

Silence again, as everyone struggled to come to terms with the enormity of the revelations.

'I think we've gone off topic,' Iain began. 'These two are still at large, and if you're saying this so-called Ben is one of the foster lads that stayed with you, then we have a lead for the police. It's just what we do with that lead, given we now know they are family?' He turned to Sarah.

'Well,' Maggie said, 'if they're who we think they are, they've both been in and out of jail for years. I met the family they were placed with years later at a foster carers' meeting. They fell out of school early. It was all downhill from there, I'm afraid. They've both been in and out of prison, Dylan more so. Sean worked in the prison kitchen, gained some sort of qualification, and has apparently tried to sort himself out a couple of times. But Dylan keeps pulling him down with him.'

Iain got to his feet. 'How's your mobile signal here, Anna?'

'Much better than the lodge's. You'll be fine.'

'Right, I'm away to call DC MacLaren, give him an update. Hopefully having their names will speed things along. At the end of the day, they set fire to the barn knowing Anna was in there, we can't ignore that.'

Sarah managed a nod towards her brother. 'You're right.' She sobbed, taking another tissue.

'And we should get going,' Maggie said rising to her feet. 'Leave these two in peace. They've a bit of talking over to do.'

Iain went to make a call and Hamish followed. Anna was left alone with Sarah and Maggie.

'Anna, love.' Maggie took Anna's hand in hers. 'I was heartbroken when your mum passed away. We were close growing up and I missed her when she left the island. Nothing was ever the same for me here, after she'd gone. Maybe, when you're feeling up to it, we could have a chat. I'd love to hear all about your life in Edinburgh, and I'm sure you'd love to hear some of the antics your mum and I used to get up to when we were young. We were close, like sisters growing up. I have some photographs, too. But only when you're ready.'

Anna struggled to hold back the tears. She gave Maggie a hug. The warmth and compassion she felt from Maggie reminded her of her own mother. And as she hugged the woman who would be able to tell her about her mother, the life they shared, and her mother's childhood on the island, Anna didn't want to let her go.

'But give Iain a chance. Hear him out. It wasn't all his fault, love. He was a broken man after your mother left. Listen to what he has to say and then make up your own mind.'

He came back in the room.

'Right, let's get going. We'll stop in Portree. Maggie you can check out of that guesthouse, you'll come and stay with us. I've to nip into the station, see DC MacLaren while we're there. Then we'll get you home, Sarah.'

Hamish offered his arm to help Sarah up.

'I'll be having a word with Anna before we go,' Sarah croaked, indignantly staying put.

Iain's eyebrow raised towards Hamish, once again. 'Aye, right, okay. Don't keep the lass too long, though.' He turned his attention to Anna. 'When you're up to it, lass'—his voice became fragile, the take-charge attitude that had just dealt with the police starting to show cracks—'perhaps we could have a chat?'

Nodding as tears filled her eyes, Anna managed, 'I'd like that.'

A relieved-looking Iain turned to leave.

'Any news, Iain? Before you go. Any updates from the police?'

'No, lad,' Iain said to Hamish, shaking his head. 'They can't even come up with a solid motive. They're presuming theft, but there was nothing taken that I can see. So it could be that Anna startled them before they had the chance to get anything out, or they'd had some other motive. Their vehicle wasn't what you would expect when robbing a place like the lodge, either. According to DC MacLaren, that is. But until they can be sure, they don't want Anna left alone—'

'Motive,' Anna interrupted. 'They did have a motive.'

All eyes were on her.

'They were looking for a painting. I'd forgotten, I could hear them speaking about it before they set fire to the barn.'

'Painting?' Iain exclaimed. 'Susanna's *Constable*, it's been in her family for years. It's worth a fortune. But how would they have known about it?'

'Because Susanna's standing in front of it in a photograph on my mantelpiece,' Maggie announced, placing her head in her hands. 'I didn't tell you, either of you,' Maggie said, glancing between Iain and Hamish, 'because I didn't want either of you to worry. But I was burgled last year. They didn't take much. I think I must have startled them. But the photo of Susannah was one of the few things they took. I presumed it was for the frame. It was one of Susanna's. She gave it to me when I left the island. I knew it was worth a fair bit, the frame, but the monetary value never mattered to me. It was a lovely image of Susanna standing in the sitting room of the lodge. The painting was hanging on the wall behind her. She wasn't long married when the photo was taken. She let me have it.' Maggie's eyes filled up. 'Iain, you and Susanna were the parents I never had. I was heartbroken when it was taken.'

Iain put a comforting arm around Maggie. 'It's okay, lass. These things happen.'

'Do you think they could have stolen your old key from you then, too?' Hamish asked.

'My old key?'

'Yes, Ben told Anna that he had borrowed the key from his mum, Maggie Sutherland.'

'But I never had a key. Not even when I lived on the island. The lodge was a hotel. It was always open. I could walk right in.'

'Well then how did he have a key?'

'Unless that was what he was up to when he was hanging around the lodge last year.'

'Could they have found it?' Sarah interjected.

'The key?' Iain asked.

'No, the painting, could they have found the painting?'

'I've no idea. I mean, they could have.' Iain shrugged. 'But I don't know where it is. I haven't seen that painting in about twenty years. I'd forgotten all about it.'

'It's in Edinburgh.'

All eyes were now on Anna.

'Edinburgh!' Iain raised his eyebrows.

'Yes, my mum left it with her letter and the photographs of you and the lodge.'

'Well, I'll be damned. Susanna gave it to Helena. Good for her. I wonder how she managed that?'

Anna stayed silent. That, she decided, was a conversation for another day.

'Well, at least we know it's safe.' Iain smiled his most relaxed smile at Anna since they'd met.

'It is, Grandad,' Anna said.

Hamish caught his mum's eye and gave her a smile.

As Hamish led Iain and Maggie to the door, Anna was aware of Sarah stiffening, her composure more in keeping with the lady she'd come to know in the cottage at the top of the hill than the kind-hearted soul who'd saved her life.

'Is everything okay, Sarah?' Anna asked after the others were outside.

'No, no it's not.'

Ageing, watery blue eyes, so reminiscent of Anna's own, teared up as Sarah braced herself for whatever she was about to say.

'What's wrong?' Anna prompted.

'It was my fault.'

'What was?'

'Your mother leaving the island, it was all my fault. I'm not proud of it, and I've had to live with the guilt, especially after…' She wiped her tears. 'I was envious of your grandmother, made her life hell, so I did, and she knew I'd make your mother's life hell, too. And most likely yours as well. I was jealous, everyone had their families and I'd lost mine. I struggled to see others happy.'

Unsure of what to say, Anna listened.

'Your grandad always got the blame for not standing up to me, but he did, and often. We had some real screamers, he and I. Always he was standing up for everyone else, never me. It took a lot of years for me to realise that, when warranted, he would stick up for me, too. He's a fair man and he did his best. I was just too wicked.'

Sarah rose from her seat as quickly as her old bones would allow. 'You know where to find me. You'll always be welcome, and the kettle will always be on. I'll not drive over here, too far for me now unless Iain gives me a lift, but I'd like to see you. I'd like to make peace.'

Wiping at her cheeks, Anna managed a nod.

'Take care of yourself, lass.' Sarah's eyes lingered on Anna before her fragile bones turned towards the door.

CHAPTER THIRTY-TWO

Hamish was making sandwiches for lunch when Anna finally broke her silence. The events of the morning had stirred a concoction of tumultuous emotions that had left her even more overwhelmed and exhausted than she'd been after the events of the previous evening.

'I get why you didn't tell me who you really were, but we need to be able to trust each other. I need to be able to trust you.'

'You can trust me.' He emptied his hands, wiping them on a towel before sitting on the edge of the sofa beside her. 'You will always be able to trust me. But it wasn't about trust. It was about protecting you from someone crooked enough to impersonate me.'

'And you thought I was part of whatever was going on?'

'I'd no idea who you were, not at first. But the thought still didn't sit right. The more I spoke to you, the more I realised you had no idea what was going on. And while you had no idea, you were safe. That guy, Dylan, showing up at the lodge, that was when I knew things could get serious. I was keeping you safe.'

Taking her hand in his, he said, 'You know how I've felt

about you. I just wanted to make sure you were safe. Not that I did a good job of that in the end.' He shuddered. 'I'm sorry, Anna. Maybe-maybe if I'd told you, last night could have been avoided.'

'Well, last night was hardly your fault. It was me who got myself caught up there in the dark with no one else around.'

'I swear, I will see the image of your trainer lying there for the rest of my life.'

As Anna took his face in her hands, he leaned in. They wrapped their arms around each other. Anna didn't want to let go, and she knew that Hamish didn't want to, either.

'Is it too soon to tell you I love you?' He blushed.

'I think we've been through enough.' She smiled at him and raised her eyebrows. 'I love you too.'

THE REST OF THE DAY HAD PASSED WITH NO FURTHER UPDATES from the police. Hamish made sure the log burner was fully stocked, and they spent the afternoon snuggling up on the sofa, watching movies and drinking hot chocolate.

Anna had a couple of naps and Rob popped in to see her before the late afternoon and evening rush hit the restaurant. He rushed around fussing over her, making sure she was keeping up with her painkillers and remembering to use the eye drops she'd been given to help with the effects of the smoke.

Hamish had then prepared one of Andy's dinners and had cleared away the dishes before joining Anna on the sofa.

The ache in Anna's ankle had been kept at bay with painkillers, but as the evening wore on, she knew she had to get her body into bed.

With Hamish following on behind, Anna manoeuvred her crutches down the hallway to her bedroom. Hamish helped her onto the edge of the bed before going to gather the rest of her things from the sofa. She retrieved her pyjamas from below her pillow and began undressing. Her top half wasn't too difficult, and she quickly swapped her fleece for a t-shirt. But removing her baggy jeans wasn't quite so easy.

'Here, let me help,' Hamish said, coming back in and taking her weight as she swapped her loose jeans for a pair of blue and green checked pyjama shorts. Goosebumps enveloped her legs.

'Are you sure you don't mind staying over?' she said.

'There's no way I'm leaving you alone with this ankle or these two on the loose.' Hamish pulled the duvet over her and sat on the edge of the bed beside her.

And as they sat together, his shoulder wrapped around hers, a calmness spread through Anna's body, reminding her it had been a long time since she'd felt as happy. Turning to kiss him, she felt relaxed and at peace. She felt safe.

He responded. His kiss more intense, more passionate, than any they had previously shared. Anna's feeling of loss, that had been so overwhelmingly raw, dissipated. Their lips lost in the moment. She pulled his body towards hers.

'Are you sure? I mean, you're not too sore.'

Her body ached, but she craved the intimacy. She wanted him, and she knew he felt the same. His warm breath on her face and the tenderness of his fingers as they caressed her cheeks were a welcome distraction from her physical pain.

His clothes fell to the floor. After helping her undress, his warm body wrapped around hers. Anna gave herself to him, freely, and with no regrets. With nothing other than a mutual understanding that they needed each other, wanted each other, and that their connection was inexplicably strong.

Their bodies were entwined; he caressed her arm while her head lay contentedly on his chest. Both lost in the moment, neither wanting to move, until an alarm sounded on Hamish's phone.

. . .

'Oh, your eyedrops. I'll go get them, it's time for your next dose.'

'I think Rob left them by the microwave,' she called after him.

While Anna shifted about in her bed, trying to get comfortable, she could hear Hamish rattling around in the kitchen.

'You alright in there?'

'Anna,' he called back, his panic obvious. 'Anna, were these letters on your microwave when Ben was here, that day he made lunch?'

'Eh, yeah, probably, why?'

'Because they've been redirected. The address to your flat in Edinburgh's on them. Not all of them, some have stickers over the address, but the ones on the top don't.'

'Oh, no.' She cupped her hands to her face. 'The last few came bundled together in a clear bag, and the sticker was on that instead.'

But Hamish was already on his phone.

'DC MacLaren, sorry to call you so late in the evening but we might have a problem.'

And as Hamish went on to inform the Detective Constable of their latest discovery, Anna was in tears. Everything her mother owned was in that flat. Unspoilt, untainted, and overwhelmingly priceless. The thought of two crooks turning it upside down to find her mother's painting was gut wrenching. She'd lost her mother. Must she lose her belongings too? It was all too much.

Hamish returned to her bedroom. 'Hey, hey, it's okay.'

His arms swept her up, holding her close as he dropped beside her. Anna trembled in his grasp at the thought of hands touching any of her mother's belongings.

Hamish pulled the duvet around them. 'DC MacLaren has

spoken with his counterpart in Edinburgh and they are sending officers over there now. They are putting a watch on the place. It turns out Dylan has violated the terms of his parole, so they're keen to nab him.' Hamish continued. 'Their thinking is that they'll have left the island last night, probably driving most if not all the way to Edinburgh overnight. They'll have lain low, intending on paying your flat a visit tonight.' He stroked her hand. 'They won't leave it any longer than tonight, as they'll know they are now up on charges of attempted murder, or murder, given they'll think you…well, you know.'

Anna attempted to slow her panicked breaths.

Hamish gave her a reassuring smile. 'All we can do just now is sit and wait. Once you're able, I'll take you to Edinburgh, but right now, there's nothing you can do. Your mum would want you to put all your efforts into looking after yourself and getting that foot and ankle better.'

His enticingly moody stare begged her to agree.

* * *

Wound up at the prospect of her flat being broken into, Anna had battled to stay awake. But her exhaustion from the events of the previous night had won out and she'd eventually drifted off. By just gone eleven, Anna had fallen asleep.

Hamish, however, was still wide awake. While Anna slept, he had busied himself tidying the kitchen and refilling the log basket before falling into the armchair beside the wood burner.

He thought about Anna, what she had been through in the last twenty-four hours, and how surreal it all felt. He'd been in love with her from a distance for so long, and now he was the one entrusted to be with her. To care for her. To protect her. They had been through so much, resulting in them becoming incredibly close in a short space of time. But last night, they had come unbearably close to losing it all.

And now, for the first time in a long time, Hamish was happy. Happy to be with the woman he loved and astonishingly grateful that his feelings had been reciprocated.

For now, though, Anna was sound asleep, and not wanting to disturb her, he pulled the blanket from the sofa loosely across his body. His phone was by his side should DC MacLaren call with an update, while the heat from the wood burner staved off the chill, allowing him to dose on and off into the early hours.

His phone ringing pulled him abruptly from a panicked dream about the ruined barns.

'Hello,' he said, his voice hoarse as he tried to fathom the time.

'Hello, Hamish. DC MacLaren here.'

'Oh, hello, do you have news?'

'I sure do. Both Sean and Dylan were apprehended last night at the property in St Bernard's Crescent. And both have been arrested on two counts of breaking and entering and attempted murder. We'll get Sean on other charges around him claiming to be you, and once we've had a chance to piece everything together properly, these charges might increase. But you can let Anna know that she can rest easy. The attempted murder charge alone will put them away for a good bit.'

'That's great news. Thank you for everything. Anna's asleep just now, but she'll probably give you a call later today.'

'You can also let Anna know there was no damage done, other than to the lock. The police pounced the minute they broke in and the property has been secured. A neighbour, name's Molly, oversaw the lock being replaced. Our guys in Edinburgh were on it, but she wanted to see for herself so she could put Anna's mind at rest. When I speak to Anna, we can sort out how she collects the new keys. But there's one other thing. Sean had a piece of paper on him. An enlarged photo-copy of a painting. Turns out it was what they were after.'

'Eh yeah, we had sussed as much,' Hamish agreed.

'Well, if that painting's in the flat, I would suggest making sure it's secure in some way. These two might not be the only two who know about it, you get what I'm saying?'

'Yes, yes, I do. I'll be sure to pass that on. Thank you for everything, DC MacLaren.

With a torrent of relief washing over him, Hamish popped his head around the bedroom door. Anna was still sound asleep.

He left her to it and went to put the kettle on. At least when she woke up he would be able to give her the good news.

CHAPTER THIRTY-THREE

After a few peaceful days together, Hamish and Anna were on their way to Portree to meet Abigail and Jamie at The Water's Edge for dinner.

Maggie had returned to Aberdeen, but not before she and Anna had enjoyed a tearful but joyous few hours sharing stories and anecdotes about Helena and the wonderful times they'd had with her.

'So how are you feeling after speaking to Iain this afternoon?'

'I feel good.' Anna beamed. 'He's nothing like I expected. He reminds me a lot of my mum, actually, which was surprisingly comforting. They're quite similar in how they think. I could tell Mum had his sense of humour, his kindness.'

'I told you. I've never known anything other than kindness from him. I mean, he'll stand up for himself or those around him, but he's steadfast and reliable.'

'He's really upset about Sean and Dylan. It's breaking his heart that their life has turned out the way it has. For Sean especially,' she said, shaking her head. 'I really must get used to calling him that. He will forever be Ben to me. But, Sean seems to have been reluctantly dragged down by his brother. Iain feels there's hope for him. But we'll see.'

'Well, knowing Iain as well as I do, I'm sure he'll find a way to help him. Dylan too, if he can. He won't let the fact that they're family go.'

'Do you know how old Iain is?'

'Eh, yeah, give me a minute, he was…he was seventy-five on his last birthday. But he's a fit seventy-five. It's the outdoor life, I reckon.' Hamish paused before continuing. 'And your dad's side, is it still a bit of a mystery? Did Iain tell you any more about that?'

'Well, he's spoken to my other grandfather. That's as much as I know. But we've got nowhere. He's not really that interested.'

'And are you okay with that?'

'Yeah, for now. I can't force it. If he doesn't want to talk, that's his choice. Iain has tried a couple of times, but he won't budge. Maybe in time he will. But to be honest, just having you, Iain, Sarah, and Maggie in my life, I feel so lucky. My little world has just exploded and I'm loving it.'

'And what about his proposition? Have you had any more thoughts?'

'It's all I can think about.'

'Me too.'

'Have you spoken to him since?'

'Yeah, but it's been about the barns. We've been sorting out the insurance claim, listing all that was lost and looking ahead at rebuilding.'

'Did you know he's decided to stay up in the cottage permanently.'

'With Sarah?'

'Yeah, apparently she's been really nice these last few days.'

'Wow, well, there's the shock of the day. I was convinced she couldn't keep up the facade.'

'Apparently, she hasn't said *feck* since the fire.' Anna laughed as she shuffled to get her foot comfortable. 'And did you know it was her bedroom that's been trashed in the lodge?'

'Yeah, she threw a tantrum the night Iain told her he was closing down the lodge and moving them up to the cottage. He couldn't bear to stay after Susanna died and Sarah couldn't bear to leave. I didn't realise why at the time, but now I can see she's lost everything and everyone she ever loved, and I know she loved living there.'

'I can't believe how my feelings towards her have changed. There is a soft side, you know, I've seen hints of it, these last few days.'

'Me too, but back to the offer. What about your photography and articles? I mean, that's your life. Wouldn't that be impacted if you took him up on his offer?'

'I would still do my photography. I couldn't not − I love it. The articles, I reckon I could keep doing too. They're only around a thousand words a piece. I reckon I could write a few in advance of opening, that way I'd never be down to the wire. What about you? What's your thoughts? I mean, wouldn't you miss working on the land?'

'Eh, no. My plan was always to be here while Iain needed me, then I'd be off.'

'Oh.'

'Don't worry, that was before I met you. And I never necessarily meant that I'd leave the island. I just didn't want to keep working on the croft. I like numbers. I like to use my brain.'

'So, you wouldn't be interested in his offer?'

'No, I'm saying I would, but—'

'But what?'

'We've just got together, and things are great. I wouldn't want to put any strain on that or do anything to spoil it.'

'Neither would I, but I have a feeling we would make a good team.'

As Anna said this, Hamish pulled up outside The Water's Edge.

He got out and ran around to the passenger side, grabbing Anna's crutches from the back seat and helping her out. 'Come on, I'll get you seated inside then I'll come out and park the jeep properly.'

'Hamish,' Anna said, 'it was Iain's idea. I'd nothing to do with it. I was just as shocked as you. But I don't want anything to spoil this either.'

His hands cupped her face; his thumbs caressed her cheeks. 'You're beautiful.' His lips met hers. 'And nothing will spoil this. We won't let it. I promise. And I'll think about it. To be honest, it excites me, too.'

Anna leaned into him, hugging him as best she could with her arms still wrapped around her crutches.

'Come on, I'll get you inside.'

HAMISH AND ANNA WERE CHATTING TO ROB WHEN ABIGAIL AND Jamie arrived. Rob was, as expected, fussing over Anna, making sure she had a spare chair to keep her foot elevated and was tucked into a corner where no one could knock it.

And as Abigail and Jamie approached the table, it was hugs all round as the four set about catching up on the events of the previous couple of weeks. Abigail was making sure Anna wasn't in too much pain while Jamie and Hamish caught up on the dramatics of the evening of the fire and the police operation that had taken place in Edinburgh.

The chatter and much-needed laughter continued into the evening, and as the last of their dinner dishes were cleared away, Rob appeared with another round of drinks.

'This round's on the house.' He winked. 'Susie, yours is a non-alcoholic cocktail so you look the part. Which reminds me, have you taken your last lot of painkillers. After food, remember?'

'Yes, Dad.'

The table erupted in laughter.

'A toast,' Abigail said, raising her glass.

As the other's raised their glasses to hers, she continued. 'Well, firstly, to Anna and Hamish, and to many happy times ahead. And to friendship.'

'Cheers' echoed around the table.

'Well, if we're toasting,' Hamish interrupted. 'Anna, I'm in if you are?'

'Seriously?'

'Yes, I think you're right. We'll make a good team.'

Abigail and Jamie looked confused as Anna threw her arms around Hamish's neck.

'I'm in.'

'What's going on, guys?' Jamie asked. 'Should we be toasting something else?'

'Eh, yes, actually. Go on, Anna. You tell them.'

She spoke through the biggest grin as she raised her glass for the others to follow. 'Iain is reopening The Old Lodge and'—she turned to Hamish—'we are going to run it, together.'

The celebrations continued, and excitement grew around the table as plans were discussed.

'Can I just butt in a minute, guys?' Jamie said. 'We've been looking for a venue that would be personal, would mean something to us.' He turned to Abigail. 'How about we are their first wedding?'

As Abigail threw her arms around Jamie, Hamish took Anna's hand in his. No words were needed.

CHAPTER THIRTY-FOUR

The following morning, Anna was sitting out on her bench, foot elevated and looking across at the view she loved. The early morning mist was rolling off the Trotternish Ridge, while the Quiraing had yet to make an appearance. Hamish had brought out blankets for her to sit on while she sipped at her coffee, and he loaded her jeep.

With a small suitcase each, a set of crutches, and a week to themselves, they were setting off for Edinburgh. Anna was going to pack up the remainder of her belongings along with her mother's desk. She had decided it was time things were switched around and the Isle of Skye officially became her permanent home.

And as her thoughts turned to her mother's letter, she embraced a sense of fulfilment alongside a feeling of gratitude for the family she had discovered, the friends she had made, and the love she knew was one to be treasured. She had fulfilled her mother's wishes...

Be strong, my darling daughter. Live life the way you always have, with courage and passion. Finish your degree. Find your way in the world and a happiness that is truly yours. Do not change who you are for anyone, and above all, love, as I will love you, always.

Abigail Returns

The Maren Bay Series - Book I

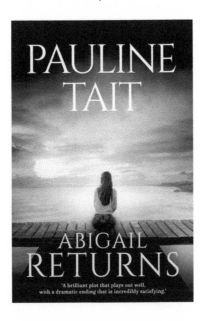

With just over a decade missing to Dissociative Amnesia, and a newly broken heart, Abigail finds herself with no choice but to return to Lochside. The supposedly idyllic home on the Isle of Skye she had fled so dramatically six years before.

And while struggling to find her way in a world she can't recall, she must battle the conflicts of the present with the shocking secrets she uncovers from her past.

Jamie's support is invaluable, but how much does he know? Greg is loving and attentive, but does he have an ulterior motive?

Meanwhile, the presence of a stranger on the island shakes Abigail to her very core. With no memory, she can only trust her instincts as she strives to build a life and a future she can call her own.

But Abigail soon discovers the stranger's trail leads far too close to home.

A riveting novel about new beginnings and second chances.

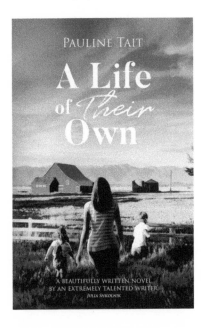

After years of living with an abusive husband, Kate embarks on a journey across America with her two young children.

Swapping the confines of their New York apartment for the Colorado mountains, Kate must learn to follow her heart and trust her instincts.

But knowing Adam will be relentless in his search to uncover her whereabouts, Kate struggles with the solitude that comes with keeping the shocking secrets of her past whilst being determined to build a new life for herself and her children.

Meanwhile, a chance encounter forces Kate to relive a past she had long left behind. And as fate takes her to Westerlakes Ranch, she must decide whether a second chance at happiness with Matthew is a risk worth taking as she strives to keep her children safe.

Can Kate ensure their freedom? Can she ensure her family will never be found?

A gripping novel about new beginnings and second chances

CHILDREN'S BOOKS BY PAULINE TAIT

AUTHOR REQUEST

Hello,

Thank you for taking the time to read **Anna's Promise**. Keep an eye out for the next book in the Maren Bay Series! Follow me on my social media sites for release announcements.

Please consider joining my mailing list here.
https://paulinetaitauthor.substack.com

I would really appreciate a review on either Amazon or Goodreads. The reviews help us indie authors a great deal.

Again, thank you for spending your precious time reading my book.

Take care,
Pauline

ABOUT THE AUTHOR

PAULINE TAIT is a novelist and children's author living and writing in Perthshire, Scotland. After working as a Pharmaceutical Technician for just over twenty years and then in Primary Literacy Support, Pauline is now writing full time.

Pauline's years of experience in working with and assessing children from Primaries one to seven, who needed extra-curricular support, then creating and delivering individual learning plans to meet their specific needs, has only fuelled her passion to encourage our younger generations in their own reading and writing. And this passion has influenced both the writing and production processes of her picture books. The covers are tactile, while care is given to the internal layouts to ensure they engage and inspire.

Pauline also writes Romantic Suspense where care is given to the credibility of her characters and their emotions. It is essential to Pauline that emotions and reactions are true to her chosen topics while the landscape and settings are truly authentic to their locations.

Sign up for news and mailings at www.paulinetait.com.

 facebook.com/ptauthor

 x.com/PTait_author

 instagram.com/tait_pauline_author

Milton Keynes UK
Ingram Content Group UK Ltd.
UKHW011332050424
440690UK00002B/251